## "Don't you ever want to marry again?"

Tina shook her head. "How could I be sure it wouldn't turn out like the first time?"

"You have to trust yourself," Wyatt said. "You have to believe you won't make the same mistake twice."

She rolled her eyes. "Do you think I haven't prayed about this? For so long I believed that no self-respecting man would want me."

"How could you possibly believe that no man would want you?"

She lifted her shoulders, muttering, "My mother was very beautiful."

"So are you."

She stared at him skeptically. Suddenly, everything changed. His gaze seemed targeted on her face, and her own heartbeat stuttered to a stop.

Oh, how she wished he was not so disturbingly attractive. That coupled with his kindness and his strength made him very nearly irresistible. But she didn't need that.

She didn't.

She didn't need a man in her life. Not even a man like Wyatt Smith.

**Arlene James** has been publishing steadily for nearly four decades and is a charter member of RWA. She is married to an acclaimed artist, and together they have traveled extensively. After growing up in Oklahoma, Arlene lived thirty-four years in Texas and now abides in beautiful northwest Arkansas, near two of the world's three loveliest, smartest, most talented granddaughters. She is heavily involved in her family, church and community.

## Books by Arlene James

### Love Inspired

#### *Three Brothers Ranch*
*The Rancher's Answered Prayer*

#### *The Prodigal Ranch*
*The Rancher's Homecoming*
*Her Single Dad Hero*
*Her Cowboy Boss*

#### *Chatam House*
*Anna Meets Her Match*
*A Match Made in Texas*
*Baby Makes a Match*
*An Unlikely Match*
*Second Chance Match*

Visit the Author Profile page at Harlequin.com for more titles.

# The Rancher's Answered Prayer

## Arlene James

LOVE INSPIRED BOOKS

Recycling programs
for this product may
not exist in your area.

ISBN-13: 978-1-335-50978-9

The Rancher's Answered Prayer

www.Harlequin.com

**Printed in U.S.A.**

For I know the thoughts that I think toward you,
saith the Lord, thoughts of peace,
and not of evil, to give you an expected end.
—*Jeremiah* 29:11

For Kay Hensley Strickland,
who has never lost her sweetness
and knows the true meanings of
family and friendship.
DAR

# Chapter One

"Maybe Uncle Dodd didn't specifically mention the house in the will because he considered it unlivable."

Wyatt Smith glanced at his brother Jacob and back to the old house in front of them. Jake had only said out loud what everyone else was thinking. Barely a speck of white paint clung to the old two-story ranch house. Its once green scalloped shingles had faded to a military gray. The front door hung slightly askew, broken glass and all, and the porch showed gaping holes where floorboards ought to be. Obviously, Uncle Dodd hadn't spent any money on upkeep in his final years, so why had he sold off all the cattle, and what had he done with the proceeds?

"We'll make do," Wyatt stated flatly, ignoring the anxious hammering of his heart.

He and his brothers could camp out, if necessary, until they got Loco Man Ranch whipped into shape, but Frankie, Jake's three-year-old son and Wyatt's nephew, needed a safe, comfortable place to live. There had to be three or four habitable rooms in this big old house. Besides, it was too late to change their minds now.

They'd sold three businesses and two houses in Houston to make this move and raise the funds necessary to restock the ranch. Two thousand acres in south central Oklahoma could support a lot of cattle, and Wyatt was determined to bring the ranch back to profitability without selling off any acreage. Sink or swim, the Smith brothers were now officially residents of Loco Man Ranch on the very outskirts of War Bonnet, Oklahoma.

He'd never dreamed that the old house would be in such a sorry state, however. This was where he and his brothers had spent many a happy summer, playing cowboy and riding horseback every day. They'd stopped coming for the summer, one by one, after high school, but they'd each made time to see Dodd at least yearly until circumstances had kept them in Houston, occupied with the deaths of their dad and Jake's wife, as well as fully taking over the family's businesses. But they were ranchers now and, like three generations of Smith men before them, their hopes lay in the land beneath their feet. God willing, they were going to put Loco Man back on the map. And put the past behind them.

At least it wasn't too hot yet. The weather in mid-April was plenty warm but not uncomfortably so.

"Let's see what we're up against," Ryder said, striding forward.

At twenty-five, Ryder stood three inches over six feet, just like his older brothers. Thirty-five-year-old Wyatt prided himself on keeping in shape, but his build was blocky, while Ryder naturally carried his hefty two hundred pounds in his powerful arms, shoulders and chest. All three brothers had dark hair and brown eyes, but Ryder's hair was straight and black, whereas Wyatt's was curly and coffee brown. Jake's slimmer build and wavy hair gave him a more polished air, especially in a military uniform, so naturally he had been the first—and thus far the only one—of the brothers to marry. Wyatt suspected that he still grieved the death of his wife, Jolene, deeply.

Handing his son to Wyatt, Jake carefully followed in Ryder's path to minimize the possibility of falling through a weak spot in the porch floor. Wyatt waited, with Frankie in his arms, at a safe distance. The existing floorboards proved solid enough. The door, however, presented a challenge.

Jake elbowed Ryder out of the way and reached through the broken glass inset, saying, "My arm's skinnier than yours."

Gingerly fumbling for several moments, he frowned, but then something clicked and the outside edge of the door dropped slightly. Jake carefully extracted his arm from the jagged hole and stepped aside so Ryder could pull the door open. Wyatt followed his brothers inside.

Red-orange sand had blown into the entry through the broken glass, dulling the dark hardwood of the foyer floor and staircase. Framed photographs covered the foyer walls, all dulled by a thick layer of dust. Many of them, Wyatt saw at a glance, were poorly framed school pictures of him and his brothers, but others showed a sturdy girl with long, chestnut brown hair and heavy eyebrows, as well as a baby photo of a wrinkled newborn in a pale blue onesie. Everything else looked the same, dusty but familiar.

Antique furniture still stood around the cold fireplace in the parlor, dimmed by time and dirt. The dining-room wallpaper looked faded, and fragile gossamer webs coated the splotchy brass light fixture above the rickety dining table. Wyatt hoped the comfortable, roomy den and Dodd's ranch office were in better shape, but the important rooms right now were the kitchen and downstairs bath.

Despite the fact that he and his brothers had run through these rooms like wild boys summer after summer, Wyatt felt as if they were trespassing. A lack of human habitation seemed to have reduced the gracious old house to a shabby pile, and made Wyatt abruptly doubt his plan. Then Ryder pushed through a swinging door into the kitchen, and suddenly Wyatt saw home.

The appliances, cabinets and countertops were hopelessly outdated, and most of the paint had worn off the familiar old rectangular table. Thankfully, however, the room appeared as habitable now as it had the last time Wyatt sat in one of those old ladder-back chairs.

While Ryder checked the water, Jake took Frankie into the bathroom, and Wyatt tried the burner on the big, white stove. Pipes banged as water started flowing. Wyatt struck a match to ignite a tiny flame.

"Looks like we're low on propane."

"Pilot light on the hot water heater must be out," Ryder said, holding his hand beneath the gushing spigot.

"We can heat water on the stove until we can see to it," Wyatt determined.

Jake returned, Frankie following and hitching up

his baggy jeans. "Storage room is full of junk, but everything seems in working order in the bathroom."

That was good news because unless Uncle Dodd had updated the plumbing, which seemed unlikely, the only shower in the house was in that downstairs bathroom.

"Check the bedrooms," Wyatt said to Ryder, who strode off at a swift clip for the staircase. "Jake, think you can find a broom?"

Before Jake could even begin to look, the sound of a vehicle arriving turned them both toward the back door.

"Company already?" Jake asked, swinging Frankie up into his arms.

"Folks around War Bonnet are friendly," Wyatt commented, "but this is ridiculous." Through the glass inset in the back door, he saw a small, white sedan pull up next to the back stoop. He walked over and threw the deadbolt, relieved that the door swung open easily.

As Wyatt watched, a curvy brunette of average height slid from behind the sedan's steering wheel. Dressed in a simple gray skirt with a bright pink, sleeveless blouse, she presented a polished, feminine picture. Her short, stylishly rumpled, cinnamon hair framed a perfectly oval face with enormous, copper-colored eyes. Though she seemed oddly familiar, Wyatt couldn't place her. Maybe she was one of the town kids who the brothers had sometimes played with. Whoever she was, she was lovely.

*If this is the War Bonnet welcoming committee*, he thought, *things are looking up already.*

Then she parked her hands on her hips, tossed her cinnamon brown head and demanded, "What are you doing in my house?"

\* \* \*

"*Your* house?"

After the week she'd had, Tina was in no mood to explain herself, especially not to some big lunk who probably thought he was God's gift to women. That's what all the good-looking ones thought, that women should fall at their big feet in stunned silence and stay that way. Well, she'd had enough of biting her tongue and hoping, praying, to be treated fairly. She'd come home—the only place she'd ever thought of as home, anyway—and here was where she intended to stay. Even if the house did look as if might fall down in a stiff breeze.

She reached into the car and grabbed her handbag. "That's right. *My* house." She lifted her chin at the big man in the doorway. "Who are you and why are you here?"

"I'm Wyatt Smith."

Oh, no. One of the Houston nephews. She should've expected this. Another man crowded into the doorway behind the first, a young boy in his arms. Both had the dark Smith hair and eyes. Wyatt slung a thumb at him. "This is my brother Jake and his son, Frankie."

Wyatt *and* Jacoby. Well, that was two of the brothers. "I suppose Ryder is also here."

Wyatt frowned. "Who *are* you?" he asked, as if he ought to know her, though they'd never met.

"I'm Tina Walker Kemp."

If the name meant anything to him, he didn't show it. He folded his arms across an impressively wide chest.

"What makes you think this house is yours, Tina Walker Kemp?"

"I don't *think* it," she said, placing one foot on the sagging bottom step. "I *know* it. My stepdaddy left me this house."

"Your stepdaddy," Wyatt repeated, his tone skeptical.

"Dodd Smith."

"Whoa!" Wyatt exclaimed. "Uncle Dodd left *us* this place."

She shook her head. "That's not what the will says."

"That's exactly what it says," Wyatt countered firmly. "And I have the will to prove it."

Tina lifted her eyebrows. "So do I."

Just then her six-year-old son, Tyler, yelled, "Mo-om, I gotta go!"

Tamping down her impatience, Tina turned back to the car and opened the door for him. They'd just driven four hours without stopping, after all, and she'd let him have that extra juice box. Besides, if the house was safe for Jake Smith's son, it must be safe for hers. She signaled for Tyler to join her, and he hopped down out of his seat, having already released his safety belt.

When Tyler reached her side, she automatically lifted a hand to smooth down the spike of reddish-blond hair that always managed to stand up. He automatically dodged her, jerking his head out of reach. The Smith brothers exchanged glances, and Jake stepped back, gesturing at Tyler.

"Come on in."

Tyler followed without bothering to look to his mother for permission. Sighing inwardly, Tina followed her son up the steps. Tyler squeezed past Wyatt, who didn't bother to move out of the way. Instead, Wyatt just stood there, challenging her with every ounce of his considerable weight. Mimicking his stance, Tina stopped on the narrow stoop, folded her arms, met his gaze squarely and purred, "Excuse me."

His shadowed jaw worked side to side as he ground his teeth, but then he stepped back and let her pass. She walked into the kitchen, both dismayed and comforted by its condition. Fortunately, she had learned long ago to keep her opinions to herself, so she made no comment. Just in case the Smith nephews thought she might be unfamiliar with the place, however, she pointed to the back hallway and addressed her son.

"Right down there, honey."

Tyler trotted off, flipping a curious wave to the youngest Smith, who hugged his father's neck with one arm and copied Tyler's gesture with the other.

"Potty," the boy said just as Tyler disappeared from sight.

"Frankie's what? Three now?" Tina asked Jake.

Nodding, Jake narrowed his eyes suspiciously before stooping to set the boy on his feet. "That's right."

The boy darted away from his father and into the arms of his uncle. Wyatt scooped him up with practiced ease. Jacoby, meanwhile, frowned at Tina.

"You sure seem to know a lot about us."

"I ought to. Daddy Dodd talked about you constantly."

"Unca Wyatt," Frankie asked, pointing a timid finger at Tina, "who's that?"

"Couldn't tell you," Wyatt replied dourly.

Tina sighed. "I told you. My name is Tina Walker Kemp. Dodd Smith was my stepfather. He left me this house and—"

"You are confused," Wyatt interrupted. "Uncle Dodd left this place to us, all two thousand acres of it."

"I'm *not* confused," Tina insisted. "Daddy Dodd sent me a paper which states clearly that the house and mineral rights to Loco Man Ranch are *mine*."

"That doesn't make any sense!" Jake erupted.

"In Oklahoma," Wyatt said, his voice low and growling, "mineral rights are separate from property rights. But nothing was ever said to me about the house *not* being part of our bequest."

Jake threw up his hands. "That's just swell."

Ignoring him, Wyatt demanded of Tina, "And just when did *Daddy Dodd* send you that paper leaving you his house and mineral rights?"

Ignoring the lump of fear that had risen in her throat—if Daddy Dodd had written a later will without telling her—Tina calmly answered, "Over two years ago, right after my divorce."

Wyatt scowled, but whether it was due to the time-line, the fact that she was divorced or the paper in her possession, Tina couldn't say. Not that it mattered. She had come home, and she had no intention of leaving. She couldn't. She had no other safe place to go.

"Now, why would Dodd leave you the house and mineral rights?" Jake wanted to know.

"Because he knew I love it here," Tina replied, sweeping aside a stray hair on her forehead. "I didn't want to leave when he and my mom split up, and I came to visit as often as I could."

Wyatt's dark eyes held hers. "You were how old when they split?"

"Almost sixteen."

"And that was how long ago?" Jake demanded. Grimacing, he added, "Sorry, you just don't look old enough to be the only stepdaughter I ever knew Uncle Dodd to have."

"Well, I am old enough," she retorted firmly. "I'm twenty-nine."

"So, thirteen years ago," Wyatt muttered. Suddenly, his eyes widened. "Wait a minute...you're Walker."

Tina couldn't help chuckling. "That's right. He called me Walker because my mother called me Tiny instead of Tina, and I had some issues with that nickname. He was the only person in the world to call me by my last name."

Wyatt finally put it together. "Your mother was Gina Walker."

"Correct." Though technically it was Gina Schultz Walker Haldon Smith Murray Becker. Gina hadn't believed in dropping the surnames of her husbands; she'd just added to them.

"That's you in the photos in the foyer," Wyatt deduced.

Tina grimaced. She'd been a tubby teenager, self-conscious about her shape, and her overbearing mother had called her Tiny in a futile effort to get Tina to slim down. When she looked in the mirror now, Tina still saw an overweight woman, but at least she knew how to dress for her figure these days.

"I think one of Tyler's baby pictures is hanging there, too," she said in a half-hearted attempt to change the subject. "At least that's where Dodd said he was going to hang it last time we were here."

"And when was that exactly?" Wyatt asked, sounding tired suddenly.

"Tyler was maybe eight months old, so about five-and-a-half years ago. Maybe a month or two longer. I think it was June." She thought a moment. "Yes, it was June. I was hoping to stay through the Fourth of July, but…"

She flashed back to the sound of the telephone ringing in the middle of the night. Her husband, Layne, had raged that she'd abandoned him when he'd needed her most and demanded that she return home. She'd stupidly gathered up her sleeping baby and hit the road, only to find that the emergency he'd referred to was nothing more than a lost commission. As his wife, accepting blame for everything that went wrong in his life had been her primary role, but at the time she'd still believed that if she was just patient and long-suffering enough, Layne would magically morph into the steady, loving husband and father she'd imagined he would be when she'd married him.

Pushing aside the unwanted memories, Tina cleared her throat. "Things were in better shape the last time I was here."

Wyatt shook his head grimly. "Wait'll we check the roof and plumbing, not to mention the electricity."

Fear tightened into a lump in Tina's stomach. The electricity had been downright scary the last time she was here, so she had no doubt that the wiring needed upgrading, but she refused to be daunted. "Doesn't matter. I'll set things to right." Somehow.

"You sound awfully sure of that," he said, "even though I stand here with a will that leaves me and my brothers everything."

She gave him her steeliest glare. "Oh, I *am* sure. One man has already taken me for everything I owned, and I'll never let that happen again."

# Chapter Two

*Well, this is a fine mess.*

Wyatt looked at the two papers in his hands, but no matter how long he stared, nothing changed. Both were dated identically and drawn up by the same attorney, Rex Billings. Sighing, Wyatt dropped the papers to the table in the Billings' ranch house kitchen and rubbed a hand across his brow. What had Uncle Dodd been thinking? And how could the lawyer let him do this? Wyatt's stomach roiled.

Dodd had mentioned Walker over the years, even though his marriage to her mother hadn't lasted long, but Tina Walker hadn't meant anything to Wyatt, so he'd tuned out the old man whenever he'd started waxing eloquent about the girl. Obviously, he should have paid better attention.

That was in the past, however, and Wyatt had known the only way to settle the current dilemma was to talk to the attorney who had apparently drawn up these ridiculous papers. Using his cell phone, he'd called the number on the will and reached one Callie Billings,

the wife of attorney and rancher Rex Billings. Now he
and Tina Kemp sat in their warm, homey kitchen sip-
ping coffee and ignoring each other. Callie, as she'd
insisted they call her, was a pretty little blonde with a
baby boy and a daughter about Frankie's age playing
quietly on the floor. Callie moved about the kitchen
with her son perched on her hip, pouring coffee and
removing cookies from the oven with one hand.

"Rex should be here any minute," she said, shifting
the baby to the other hip. The front door opened, and
Callie smiled brightly.

They heard two thumps, followed by silence. A few
seconds later, the swinging door between the dining
room and kitchen opened, and a tall, dusty cowboy
padded into the space on his stocking feet. The little
girl on the floor jumped up and ran to greet him, throwing her arms around his thighs.

"Hello, darlin'." While Callie went to him, baby and
all, he explained the situation. "My boots were filthy
so I yanked them off. Now I need to wash my hands."
Holding his hands away from them, he kissed the baby,
then his wife.

Wyatt couldn't help but feel envious. He'd expected
to be married and settled into family life by now himself, but somehow it just hadn't happened. Billings hurried to the sink to wash his hands. Finally, he turned
back to the table.

"You must be Wyatt Smith."

Wyatt stood and put out his hand. "That's right.
Thank you for seeing us on such short notice."

Shaking hands with Wyatt, Billings glanced at Tina
and nodded. He looked to his wife then. "Honey, I've

been dreaming about your coffee and cookies. Set me up." He sat down at the table. His daughter crawled up into his lap.

"Daddy, can I hab cookies?"

"*Have* cookies. What does Mama say?"

"Ask you."

"Then you can have *one* cookie."

"Yay!"

Callie had the cookie wrapped in a napkin by the time Billings set the girl on her feet.

"Sit on your blanket and eat," Callie instructed gently, as she poured another cup of coffee.

"We were sure sorry to hear about Dodd's passing," Billings began as Callie set the coffee in front of him.

"Thank you," Wyatt and Tina said at the same time.

Wyatt frowned at her. She spoke as if she were Dodd's next of kin. Then again, Dodd had spoken fondly of her over the years, though if he'd told his nephews nearly as much about her as he had apparently told her about them, they hadn't been paying attention.

"I was sorry that Dodd left instructions not to have a service," Billings went on, lifting his coffee cup. "It would have been well attended. He was much liked around War Bonnet."

"I appreciate you saying so," Wyatt told the other man, cutting a glance at Tina, who nodded and pressed her lips together as Callie placed a platter of cookies and three small plates in front of them.

"Now," Billings said, "how can I help you?"

"There seems to be some confusion about my uncle's will," Wyatt explained, passing the papers to Billings.

Rex swallowed some coffee and glanced over the

papers across the rim of his cup before stacking them on the table at his elbow. "No confusion. Dodd was very certain about what he wanted and how he wanted to do it."

"I don't understand."

Rex shrugged and reached for a cookie. "Your uncle wanted Ms. Kemp to have the house and the mineral rights. You and your brothers get everything else."

"I told you," Tina crowed triumphantly. She reached a hand across the table toward Rex. "I'm Tina Walker Kemp, by the way."

"Not Mrs. Smith, then."

Both Wyatt and Tina reacted at the same time. "No!"

Billings shot a glance at Wyatt before shaking Tina's hand. Then he released her and placed some cookies onto plates for her and Wyatt. "Eat up."

Tina nibbled, but after one bite of cookie, the world as a whole seemed a lot more palatable to Wyatt.

"Mmm. You should market these," Wyatt told Callie Billings, shaking a cookie at her.

"Don't even joke about it," Rex protested. "She has enough to do with me, these kids, my dad and helping her own father run his businesses."

"If you're looking to sell Loco Man," Callie said to Wyatt, "Rex and my dad might be interested in buying. You may know my father. Stuart Westhaven."

"The banker?"

"Among other things."

"Beware an ambitious businesswoman," Rex put in, shaking his head. "Always looking to expand." He reached out and pulled Callie close to him, kissing her soundly.

Envy knocked around inside Wyatt's chest again. Unbidden, his gaze stole to Tina Walker Kemp, who stared morosely at her empty plate as if wishing for the return of her cookie or perhaps another. Frowning at himself, Wyatt focused his mind on the subject at hand.

"We're not interested in selling," he stated firmly, though once his brothers heard that Tina's claim was real, they might have other ideas. Blanking his face, he asked, "You wouldn't know where we might rent a place to stay, would you? There's four of us, including my nephew, Frankie."

Rex shook his head. "Not offhand."

Wyatt grimaced before he could stop himself. "Something affordable to buy, then. Preferably on the east side of town."

"Lyons might have something for sale."

"Dix told me they sold that house they remodeled," Callie put in. "Saw him and Fawn at the grocery store."

"Well, there's a realtor in town. He'll know," Rex said casually. "I think your uncle was expecting y'all to share, though."

"Share!" Tina yelped, glaring at Wyatt as if he'd suggested the idea.

"Everyone knows the old house needs some work," Callie pointed out. She looked to Wyatt then, adding, "Even if you and your brothers aren't up to that, you could pay rent so Ms. Kemp could afford to hire Lyons and Son." She smiled at Tina. "They do excellent work, by the way."

*Rent.* Wyatt ground his teeth. His business plan didn't allow for rent, let alone buying a house for himself and his family. He especially did not like the idea of paying rent to live in what was rightly Smith property, but what was the option? Staying in the bunkhouse?

"What about the outbuildings?"

"They're yours," Rex told him. "Dodd was very intentional about it. The house and the mineral rights go to Ms. Kemp. Everything else goes to you and your brothers. Technically, you own the ground that the house sits on."

Well, that tipped the equation in his favor. Wyatt smiled cunningly at Tina Walker Kemp. "Maybe we can work something out."

She folded her arms mulishly, but Wyatt saw the worry in her big bronze eyes. Suddenly, he wanted to reassure her, promise not to pull the ground out from under her and her son. Literally. But the interested gazes of Rex and Callie Billings squelched the impulse.

Besides, whatever Uncle Dodd's foolish intentions had been, Wyatt meant to make a home on Loco Man Ranch for himself, his brothers and his nephew—Tina Kemp or no Tina Kemp.

Something told him that she would take nothing less than her due.

So be it.

*Well, wasn't that just like a man?*

Tina had never met a man who could keep his word. In the end, even Daddy Dodd had disappointed her. What did he think he was doing, leaving every square inch of the land to the Smith brothers and only the house that sat upon it to her? All right, the house *and* the mineral rights, for whatever that was worth.

At this point, she was afraid to hope. Where had hope ever gotten her? As the thought slid through her mind, she quickly followed it with a prayer.

*Sorry, Lord. I'm just confused. And frightened. Lord, please, there must be some way to make this work, some way I can keep Tyler with me.*

She'd snorted with derision when her ex-husband, Layne, had informed her that he intended to sue for custody of their son. Then his attorney had contacted her, and suddenly the threat had become all too real. Dodd had died only days before. In her grief and panic, she'd gone searching for the copy of the will he'd sent her. At the time, it had seemed as if Dodd had reached down from Heaven and handed her the answer to her problems. She could leave a job that demanded too much of her time and go home to Oklahoma with her son.

She hadn't given a thought to the land, only to the house. In the back of her mind, she'd sort of assumed that the ranch would go on as it always had, with Dodd's longtime foreman, Delgado, at the helm and reporting to the nephews. She'd never expected them to leave the big city of Houston, Texas, for the tiny town of War Bonnet, Oklahoma. She certainly hadn't expected them to take over *her* house.

She'd decided that she would open a bed-and-breakfast. With the nearest motel room at least 40 miles away, Dodd had often put up folks visiting War Bonnet. That neighborliness was one of the things that her mother, Gina, had disliked so much about small-town life.

Tina smiled wanly at Callie, wishing they had more

in common. Perhaps they soon would. Callie obviously placed making a home for her family at the top of her list, but she was also a businesswoman. The fact that Callie and her husband so clearly adored each other was the big difference between her and Tina. Well, that and the fact that Callie's house wasn't falling down around her.

Tina wondered if cashing in her small 401(k) to finance this had been wise, but what choice had she had?

Wyatt pushed back his chair and rose to his feet, stretching his hand across the table to Rex. The two men shook as if they were longtime friends.

"We would be most grateful," Wyatt was saying. "It's been a long time since I was on a horse, and I've never bought a cow in my life."

"We're just about through tagging and cutting the calves," Billings said, hooking his thumbs in the front pockets of his dusty jeans. "Give me another a few days, and we'll get at solving your livestock problem."

Callie chuckled. "Be warned. Rex especially loves to shop for horses."

"No one's more surprised by that than I am," Rex told her, hooking an arm about her waist and pulling her close again.

She laughed and said to Wyatt, "My husband has more in common with you than you know, Mr. Smith. He left Tulsa and a stellar law practice to come back here and help out when his father was ill. Then he found that the city no longer had any appeal."

It was obvious to anyone with eyes what had kept Rex in War Bonnet. Tina wanted to be happy for the couple, but to her shame she found that she could only be envious.

Had Layne ever looked at her like that? She highly doubted it. Why hadn't she been sensible enough to realize that the only thing about her that had attracted him was her attraction to him?

She had promised herself that she wouldn't follow in her mother's footsteps, flitting from husband to husband as if she were a bee darting from flower to flower. Yet, she had been the bee and Layne the flower in their relationship.

She wouldn't make that mistake again.

Thankfully, she had her son, and he was all she needed. She hadn't been enough for her own mother, and Tina was determined that her son would never feel that cold realization. Her father, whom she'd seen only a few times in her life, was little more than a name to her.

Tina wondered guiltily if she should relent and allow Layne to have custody of Tyler, but then she recalled her ex snarling at her that he would take everything she valued if she dared divorced him. He'd managed it, too, with everything and everyone but their son.

Dazedly, she felt a hand on her elbow. She didn't remember coming to her feet, but suddenly she realized that their meeting had ended. Wyatt now seemed determined to escort her from the premises. To cover her confusion and dismay, Tina subtly tugged free of him, smiled at their hostess and nodded at Rex before turning toward the door.

"Thank you for your time," she murmured.

Wyatt held open the door, saying something about

paying Rex for the consultation. Thankfully, Rex insisted that no payment was necessary. Relieved, she
tried not to look at Wyatt's big, broad hand as she
walked through the door. They moved through the dining and living rooms and into the foyer, Rex following in his stocking feet. Wyatt opened the front door
for her. She pushed wide the screen and crossed the
porch, stepping down onto the beaten dirt path that ran
through the post oaks to the bronze-colored, double-
cab pickup truck parked on the side of the red dirt road.

That truck was more luxurious than any vehicle
Tina had ever ridden in. An electronic *beep* signaled
that Wyatt had released the locks. Tina yanked open
the door and stepped up onto the running board that automatically slid out from beneath the truck. She buckled her safety belt and waited for Wyatt to get in on
the driver's side.

He started the engine and turned on the air condi-
tioning. Then he spoke. "Looks like we're stuck with
each other."

Stuck. That about summed up her life. She'd been
stuck with her mother and then four subsequent stepfa-
thers. No doubt Gina would have added another name
to her long list if she hadn't tripped on the trailing
hem of her dressing gown and fallen down a flight of
stairs, breaking her lovely neck in the process. That's
what had prompted Tina to accept Layne's marriage
proposal, only to find herself stuck with a handsome
chameleon who'd ultimately cheat on her.

She'd left Layne and met with a lawyer the next
day. Layne had never again allowed her back into the
house. With no choice but to find immediate employ-

ment, she'd found herself stuck in the job of secretary to a demanding real estate developer who expected her to toil the same endless hours that he worked.

Now here she was, stuck with the Smith brothers.

"Oh, Lord, why?" she prayed, not realizing that she'd spoken aloud until Wyatt sighed.

"When He answers, be sure to let me know."

## Chapter Three

He didn't answer. God never seemed to answer her prayers.

She'd prayed that her mother's marriage to Dodd Smith would last. As easygoing and affable as he was hardworking, Dodd had been Tina's friend as much as her stepfather. After only nine months, however, Gina had declared herself bored beyond bearing and ended the marriage.

None of her prayers for her own marriage had been fulfilled, either, with one exception. Her son.

Now Layne wanted to take him, too.

For Tyler, she had left Kansas City and come here. For Tyler, she would put up with the Smith brothers and do everything in her power to make this move work.

"I'll trade you housing for help fixing up the house," she proposed, glancing from brother to brother.

She had taken a seat at the table in the dusty kitchen. The brothers had positioned themselves around the room. Wyatt leaned against the sink, his arms folded. Jake stood at the edge of the hallway as if listening to his son playing with hers in the laundry room, where the boys were taking turns rolling small cars into the corner of the sadly sloping floor. Ryder had hopped up to sit on the counter between the sink and the stove. Ryder Smith was only a few years her junior, but he had a sweetness about him that made him seem younger.

"I don't mind helping out," he said.

Wyatt shot him a glare. Ryder shrugged. "And once the house is fixed up, what then?" Wyatt wanted to know.

Tina lifted her chin. "You'll need to find other accommodations. I plan to turn this house into a bed-and-breakfast."

Jake snorted, and Wyatt rolled his eyes. Ryder, however, lifted his head in surprise and blurted, "Well, that makes sense. Uncle Dodd used to take in folks who came to visit family and friends in War Bonnet."

Tina could have kissed him. She noticed Wyatt again glared at Ryder. She knew instinctively that Wyatt was the brother she had to convince.

"We have a ranch to get going," he stated flatly. "We don't have time to remodel an old house."

"And we're going to live where while we're getting the ranch going?" Jake wanted to know.

"We can convert the bunkhouse into our living quarters." Wyatt turned his glare on Tina. "The outbuildings belong to us."

"I never said otherwise."

"Okay," Jake interjected, leaning a shoulder against the wall. "So, where do we live while we're converting the bunkhouse? It hasn't been used in decades, so I doubt there's even plumbing."

"Besides, why does it take all three of us to work the ranch when we don't even have any cattle?" Ryder wanted to know.

"We'll have cattle soon," Wyatt insisted, shifting his feet. "Rex Billings is going to help us find the livestock we need, including horses."

"You and Delgado can handle that, can't you?" Jake asked. "Meanwhile, I can work on the bunkhouse and Ryder can start putting this place to rights."

"What do a mechanic and a fight—" He broke off midword and scrubbed a hand over his face, heavily shadowed now with a day's growth of beard. "What do you and Ryder know about construction?"

"We know as much about carpentry as we do about ranching," Ryder put in softly. "I don't say we can do everything that's needed, but we can do a lot."

"Actually," Jake said, "we know *more* about construction than ranching. You forget that I remodeled my own house while Jolene was deployed and that Ryder worked in construction before…"

Tina glanced between the brothers, first at Ryder's bowed head, then at Wyatt, who studied his youngest brother with undisguised concern, and back at Jake. She saw sadness in all of them, deep, heavy sadness. But why? Some time ago, Dodd had mentioned that Jake's wife had died, but Tina sensed something else going on here.

Wyatt shook his head, then he looked at her and nodded. "Fine. Ryder will work for you while Jake takes care of the bunkhouse and I get the ranch started."

She doubted she would get a better offer. Still… She made a final demand.

"And you agree to deed me the land that the house sits on."

Wyatt's dark gaze held hers for several long, tense moments. "We'll see. I might just buy you out."

Surprised by the suggestion, Tina again glanced around the room. Apparently, Jake and Ryder were equally surprised.

"What makes you think I'll agree to that?"

He shrugged. "Maybe you don't have the money to renovate this old house."

He was right, but she'd learned a few things over the years, and she did have some connections to draw on. She knew where to find the very best bargains on building supplies and could call in a few favors.

"I'll manage," she told him.

"What about meals?" Jake wanted to know.

"I can cook," Tina drawled, "if that's what you're asking."

Jake looked pointedly at Wyatt, who seemed to require a moment to tamp down his irritation before saying, "We'll buy the groceries if you'll cook the meals."

"Done."

He waved a hand. "I suggest we figure out who gets what bedroom and settle in."

Jake pushed away from the wall. "Frankie and I can share."

"Actually," Ryder said, "we may all have to share. Some of the rooms are empty of furniture. Two are uninhabitable. The window is missing in one of the rooms, and either the roof leaks or something's chewed through the ceiling in another."

Dismayed, Tina gasped. All eyes turned her way.

"What do you mean the window is missing?"

"I mean that it's gone." Ryder spread his hands, palms up. "Including the casing."

"And something chewed through the ceiling?"

"Well, there are tiny teeth marks around the opening."

Wyatt let loose a long, gusty sigh. "Okay. Get up to the attic and see what you can find. But watch yourself. The last thing we need is for anyone to get hurt. Jake, you and Ms. Kemp look at the other rooms and decide who goes where. I'll start unloading our gear."

"Call me Tina," she corrected. If they were going to be living in the same house, it seemed only right to be on a first-name basis.

Wyatt inclined his head, laying a hand to his chest. "You can call me Wyatt."

Jake lifted his hand. "It's Jacoby, but everyone calls me Jake."

Tina knew this, but she simply nodded.

"And I'm Ryder," the younger brother said, smiling.

"Dodd told me all about the three of you," Tina said, smiling in return.

"That's more than we can say for you," Wyatt muttered, moving toward the door.

Ignoring him, Tina pushed back her chair and stood. With so much to do and so much at stake, she couldn't afford to worry about anything else. Time to get to work.

She and Jake spoke to the boys, warning them to stay in the house out of harm's way while the adults arranged their living quarters. Frankie nodded compliantly, but as usual Tyler argued.

"Why can't we go outside?"

"Because we haven't had a chance to look around yet," Tina told him. "It's too dangerous until we know the outbuildings are all clear of vermin and the porch is roped off."

"Aw, I ain't scared of no vermin," Tyler sneered.

"You should be," Jake said. "Rats, squirrels, raccoons and skunks often carry rabies."

"What's rabies?"

"A very serious illness," Jake explained.

"I don't care," Tyler grumbled mulishly.

"I hope you don't mind shots then, because rabies will keep you in the hospital for lots of shots," Jake informed him.

Tyler frowned, considering this. Finally, he said, "I better make sure Frankie 'n' me don't get rabies."

"I'd appreciate that," Jake replied gravely, but Tina saw by the twinkle in his dark eyes that he was amused.

"Call out if you need us," Tina instructed. "We'll just be upstairs."

Tyler nodded and went back to rolling the toy car, accompanied by the sound effects of a revving engine and screeching tires. Tina followed Jake from the room, aware that he silently chuckled, his shoulders shaking with mirth.

"Boys," he commented softly when she fell into step beside him. "I think they're all born with a certain amount of stubborn pride."

Tina sighed. "I think Tyler got more than his fair share."

"Oh, I wouldn't worry about him. He's played well and been very patient with Frankie today."

She smiled her thanks for that and wondered why it was so much easier to like Jake than his older brother. The same seemed to be true of Ryder. A pity that Wyatt was the better looking one.

Most attractive, least likeable. Thankfully.

The last thing she needed was any sort of romantic entanglement. She had long since vowed that she would not follow her much-married mother's path. The only thing on her mind now would be creating a safe, stable home for her son. She'd do whatever she had to do to make that happen. Then Layne and his lawyer could take a hike.

Resolved, she accompanied Jake upstairs to see what Herculean tasks awaited her.

"The last thing we need is possums in the house," Wyatt muttered, staring at Ryder, who was covered in dust from his head to his shoes. He had cobwebs in his black hair, which he attempted to brush out with his fingers.

They'd all crowded into the upstairs hallway to hear what Ryder had found in the attic. This day just kept getting worse and worse, in Wyatt's estimation. First they found the house in sorry condition. Then they'd learned that Tina Kemp actually owned the thing. Now they were obligated to help her fix it up, critters included.

"Could be worse," Ryder reported. "I found evidence of bats."

Tina surprised Wyatt by letting out a frightened *eep*. She hugged herself and asked, "Will they come back?"

"Hope not. I've blocked every entry point to the attic

that I could find, including the hole in the ceiling. I'll cover up the empty window, and tomorrow I'll fix the ceiling, but the roof will need to be addressed before long because I also saw evidence of leaks up there."

Tina muttered something under her breath, but Wyatt chose to ignore it.

"Good work," he said to Ryder. "You and I can take the room with twin beds. Jake and Frankie can share one of the full beds." He turned to Tina. "That just leaves you and Tyler."

"We'll share my old room for now. There's only a twin bed, but I can make up a pallet on the floor."

Wyatt had brought up her many suitcases, so he now carried them to the room with the pink gingham wallpaper, making two trips. Some of the bags had to stay out in the hall.

"I can't vouch for the bedding," he told her, as she began positioning suitcases around the room and opening them.

"I brought my own."

"Thank God," he said. "All we brought are sleeping bags, and I doubt Jake would want to share one with Frankie even for a single night. Kid's a mini tornado in his sleep, all flailing arms and legs." He chuckled, thinking of the nights he'd spent with Frankie when both Jake and Jolene had been deployed. If not for the overwhelming relief of having his brother return safely from the war zone, Wyatt might have been jealous of his brother for taking Frankie home with him. Then Jolene had been killed in a training exercise just weeks after returning home, and Wyatt's envy had turned to grief.

Tina looked at Wyatt, her expression solemn. "Are you the kind of man who normally thanks God?" she asked.

Wyatt blinked and nodded. "I am." To his surprise, her coppery gaze softened a bit before she turned away, a pair of worn jeans and a faded red tank top in her hands.

"Good to know. Now if you'll excuse me, I'd like to change. Then we can strip the beds and haul the mattresses outside to beat the dust out of them."

Why hadn't he thought of that? "Of course." He backed out of the room and caught Jake by the elbow as he was heading downstairs, informing him of their latest chore.

While he and Jake manhandled the mattresses down to the porch to whack the dust out of them, Tina wiped down and swept out all seven rooms upstairs. Thankfully, she found additional bedsheets in the linen closet at the end of the hall. After tumbling them in the dryer to remove dust and anything else that might have found its way into the folds, she made up the beds. In the end, the sleeping bags weren't needed, so Wyatt had her use those to make a comfortable pallet for Tyler.

Unfortunately, the dryer repeatedly threw the breaker in the outdated junction box in the laundry room. Worse, more than one outlet sparked noticeably when they tried to use it. So, after the sheets were refreshed, they turned off the electricity. Considering the poor wiring, a portable generator—if they could even find one—didn't seem wise.

"Guess I'd better put an electrician at the top of my

list," Tina said tiredly as the waning sun threw shadows across the room.

"Looks like it," Wyatt agreed. "We can manage with flashlights for a while. Tomorrow I'll order some propane and see about changing the utilities into—"

"*My* name," Tina said flatly, dropping down onto the chair.

Wyatt sighed but remained silent.

"For the record," she went on, looking as weary as Wyatt felt, "I intend to divide two of the bedrooms upstairs into bathrooms. That will leave five bedrooms, though I intend to turn one of those into a sitting room that can be shared by the back two bedrooms. Just so you know."

"That leaves just four bedrooms for six people."

"Eventually, Tyler and I will sleep downstairs."

"In what? The den?"

"The den can be divided," she pointed out. "It's an enormous room. And there's the junk room."

Man, he hated this added complication. He and his brothers already had enough to deal with. They didn't need all this confusion, what with rooms being divided all over the house.

*Lord, show me how to get through this*, he silently prayed. *Don't let me say and do things I'll regret. We need the ranch to work for us.*

"Is there any food?" Tina asked, running a hand through her thick, spiky hair. "If so, I'll start supper as soon as the water is heated."

She had two huge pots of water on the stove for the boys' baths, but the adults would have to make do with cold showers tonight.

"I'm afraid there's not much here," Wyatt informed her. She looked too tired to cook, anyway, but he didn't say so. "Jake offered to head into town to pick up burgers for supper, if that's all right with you."

"Works for me. I'll hit the grocery store tomorrow and buy some food."

Wyatt's stomach applauded that plan. He just hoped she could actually cook. If not, they'd be back to living on canned goods, cereal and the limited fare from the town's single eatery. Wyatt had fond memories of the old diner, but he wouldn't want to eat there three times a day.

"You didn't seem to bring much in the way of housekeeping supplies," Ryder commented, rubbing his dark head with a thin towel.

She shook her head, her short chestnut hair flopping over her eyes. Pushing aside the glossy strands, she said, "Didn't have much to bring, but surely Dodd left enough pots and pans to see us fed."

"I wouldn't count on it, but we should have everything you need," Wyatt told her, heading toward the bathroom. "In fact, I don't know where we're going to put all the furniture."

"You're moving in furniture?" Tina squawked in obvious surprise.

Actually, they had enough furniture for two households, but he kept that information to himself for the moment.

"Don't get in a huff," he said, coming to a halt. "The moving company will store our things until the bunkhouse is ready. You'll have plenty of room for your furniture." That came off as surly, which was not his intention. Before he could soften his remarks, however, she wearily lifted the back of her forearm to her brow.

Sighing, she muttered, "I don't have any furniture. This is it for us."

Wyatt frowned. "What? Not even a TV?"

She shook her head again. "Nearly everything was rented, and what wasn't, I sold."

Suddenly, Wyatt felt guilty because he'd silently grumbled that she'd brought more suitcases than he and his family together.

"Besides," she said, keeping her gaze averted, "I didn't have room for anything else."

That was the truth. The car had been stuffed. He'd assumed that the bulk of her goods would follow, but now he remembered something she'd said earlier.

*One man has already taken me for everything I owned, and I'll never let that happen again.*

Apparently, she'd left her marriage with very little. Wyatt had been under the impression that belongings were divided equitably during a divorce. Maybe she and her husband hadn't acquired much, but she and her ex should have had at least four or five years to acquire a few furnishings.

Had her ex sent her and her son into the world without the necessities? Wyatt frowned at the thought. Not that it was any of his business. Besides, he disliked the curiosity that her situation aroused in him. In fact, he disliked her, though he couldn't honestly say why.

This situation wasn't her fault, after all. When it came right down to it, what she did with this house was no business of his. The house and everything in it belonged to her. But what on earth had Dodd been thinking when he'd created this mess?

Wyatt hurriedly showered and dressed. He decided not to shave, despite his scruffy appearance. Staying clean-shaven was a near impossibility with his heavy beard, and he wasn't eager to attempt a smooth shave with cold water. Plus, with daylight fading, he needed to leave time for the others to clean up.

Tina was next and dressed in fresh jeans and a baggy T-shirt. With her hair wet and her subtle makeup scrubbed away, she could have passed for sixteen. For the first time, her hair looked as dark as her gracefully arched brows.

She had the most amazing skin he'd ever seen. Her big, almond-shaped eyes were a bright shade of light brown, somewhere between amber and copper. Wyatt had to work at not staring.

Relieved when she went back into the bathroom to scrub the tub, he got Frankie ready for his bath. Then he helped Ryder carry in the hot water and fill the tub. After adding cool water to achieve the perfect temperature, Tina bathed the boys together and dressed them in pajamas.

With his dad gone to get dinner, Frankie crawled up into Wyatt's lap at the old kitchen table while Tina scrubbed the table top. The odd domesticity of the situation felt both peculiar and satisfying at the same time.

He hadn't shared a house with a woman in the nearly twenty years since his mother, Frances, had died, leaving him a fifteen-year-old with younger brothers, aged ten and five, to care for. Their father had been devastated after the auto accident that had taken his wife.

Once he'd recovered from his own injuries, Albert Smith had buried himself in work and grief. The job of raising his younger brothers had chiefly fallen to Wyatt. Long before a heart attack had taken their father, almost six years ago now, Wyatt had assumed the role of family patriarch.

Jake's wife, Jolene, had been the only significant female influence to enter the Smith realm in all the years since Frances's death. As a soldier, Jolene had been as much warrior as woman in Wyatt's estimation, so in many ways, she'd felt like one of the guys.

He couldn't think of Tina Kemp that way.

It would be best then, Wyatt told himself, if he didn't think of Tina at all.

As he entertained Frankie, Wyatt surreptitiously watched as Tina ruffled her damp hair with a towel. Women with short hair didn't usually appeal to him, but Tina couldn't have appeared more feminine.

The woman wasn't just lovely—she was a beauty, which meant that this living arrangement was going to be a real trial.

## Chapter Four

Jake finally returned home with supper, and Tina set out everything and got the boys situated at the table. Tall for his age, Tyler required no help reaching his food. Frankie, however, needed a lift. She found a small plastic tub sturdy enough to serve as a booster seat.

According to his brothers, Jake was famous for his hot showers, so no one was surprised that he came out shivering in his jeans and white T-shirt. Wyatt and Ryder laughed at him, bantering about bathing conditions in Afghanistan and the average military barracks. Tina was not surprised to learn that Jake was former military. Something in his manner marked him as a soldier; yet, Wyatt remained the undisputed head of this family.

Once they were all seated, Wyatt bowed his head. Tina froze in the act of unfolding the paper wrappings on her burger. She caught Tyler's glance and put her hands together to show him that they were going to pray, something she'd let slide recently. Frankie obviously had been through this routine many times. Fold-

ing his chubby hands, he bowed his little head along
with his father and uncles.

Wyatt glanced up at her. "Uh, would you like to
say grace?"

Tina took the opportunity to prompt her son. "Tyler,
maybe you'd like to pray over our meal tonight."

Grimacing, Tyler bowed his head and intoned the
familiar words. "God is great. God is good. Thank
You, Lord, for this food. And maybe we can go back
home soon. Amen."

"We are home, son," Tina corrected softly.

That unenthusiastic prayer stuck in Tina's head as
she ate her meal and the Smith brothers talked over the
next day's plans. With the house a wreck and the cattle
gone, she couldn't help wondering why they were even
here. She thought about explaining her own situation
and appealing to the brothers' compassion in the hope
that they would simply return to Texas. In truth, however, she needed their help. Actually, if not for Wyatt,
she'd be quite happy with the situation.

What was it about him, she wondered, that disturbed
her so?

It didn't matter. She couldn't see any option other
than to follow through with her plan. Maybe Wyatt
would be too busy with the ranch to waste time making her life difficult.

Vain hope, that. He was a man, wasn't he?

On the other hand, despite the fiasco of the wills,
Daddy Dodd had been a caring, stalwart friend when
she'd most needed one. Maybe his nephews were more
like him than first impressions had indicated.

Strange, but that thought brought neither hope nor

relief. She could only pray that Wyatt would be so dili-
gent about getting the ranch into shape that he stayed
out of her business. Too weary to worry about it, she
and Tyler retreated to their room as soon as it was dark.
She slept surprisingly well, waking far later than usual
to find Ryder frying eggs and bacon that Jake had jour-
neyed back into town to purchase. Thankfully, Wyatt
had already departed on ranch business, according to
Ryder, who had no idea when Wyatt would return.
Tina silently thanked God for that small blessing, and
sat down with pencil and paper to discuss with Ryder
what repairs were most urgently needed.

Wyatt shook the dusky hand of the man he had ever
only known as Delgado. Relief bolstered his hope.
They'd agreed to meet at the diner in War Bonnet,
where both had enjoyed a decent breakfast and excellent coffee, while ignoring the obvious interest of the
locals. They'd quickly come to terms about Delgado's
continued employment.

"I'm very glad to get you back at Loco Man," Wyatt
said as he pushed through the glass door to the side-
walk.

"I am glad again to work for a Smith," Delgado replied.

The smiling vaquero's once dark hair had turned to
a dull salt-and-pepper shade that would soon be more
salt than pepper, but he'd maintained his lean, ropy
strength.

"Do you have time to drive around the ranch with
me?" Wyatt asked. "Rex Billings has offered to take

me to a sale barn in Tulsa to purchase horses in a few weeks, so we can't ride."

"Yeah, *sí*," Delgado said with a grin. "We take my old truck. No reason to batter yours. No one better with horseflesh than a Billings, but we had ATVs in the barn, unless Dodd sold those, too."

"There are two," Wyatt confirmed, falling into step beside the ranch foreman, "but they don't seem to run."

"They pro'ly just need gas and spark plugs," Delgado surmised.

"I'll have Jake look at them. He's our mechanic. Meanwhile, your truck will do fine."

This wouldn't be his first time riding with Delgado behind the wheel. Crazy as it seemed, he'd once taken the passenger seat as Delgado had raced his battered old truck across a bumpy pasture while Uncle Dodd had roped a particularly troublesome stud from the truck bed. That was not a feat Wyatt intended to repeat, but because of it he had no qualms about letting Delgado take the wheel.

"Meet me at the house," Wyatt instructed, "and we'll go from there."

"Yeah, *sí*."

Wyatt chuckled at the familiar double assent. As a young boy, he'd assumed that *ya-sí* was the Spanish word for *yes*. Only later had he realized that Delgado frequently spoke in a combination of English and Spanish.

A few hours later, neither of them could manage a smile. As he brought the dusty old pickup truck to a stop beside the house, Delgado's expression registered as much confusion as Wyatt's. Dimly, Wyatt noted that in the intervening hours Ryder had repaired the floor of the porch, rehung the front door and replaced the broken glass pane. Wyatt's immediate concern, however, was the puzzling condition of the ranch.

They'd driven past fenced acreages sown in what appeared to be a variety of grasses. Those large plots, some of them thirty and forty acres, didn't even have gates to let cattle in to graze. Some were irrigated with portable, aboveground systems powered by rackety old windmills. Some were not.

"Was Dodd experimenting?" Wyatt mused. "Could he have been trying to figure out which grass was most hardy and would best support cattle?"

Delgado shrugged and shook his head. "He never say. When the worms got the cattle, some had to be put down. The rest we treat and sell. Then he start dragging in old windmills and drilling wells. 'Times change,' he say. And he start the grass, many kinds. He hire that Pryor kid to do it, the one with the farming equipment. And we build fence roun' the grass."

"Fences without gates," Wyatt murmured. "It doesn't make sense."

"Some say he lost his mind," Delgado reported bluntly, "that he was loco like his great-grandfather, but I think no."

The legend was that Wyatt's great-great-grandfather had illegally paid others during the land rush to stake claims to the vast acreage that eventually became the Smith ranch. Then, when authorities called him on the scheme, he'd pretended not to understand the problem, no matter how it was explained to him, leading others to label him loco or insane. Wyatt somehow doubted that a reputation for insanity would have swayed the authorities, even back then, to simply allow Great-Great-Grandpa Smith to keep his ill-gotten gains. Nevertheless, he'd named the ranch Loco Man, with an apparent tongue-in-cheek reference to the rumors.

"I just wish I knew what Dodd was thinking," Wyatt admitted on a sigh.

"So, we run cattle at Loco Man again, yeah, *si*?" Delgado asked.

"We are most definitely going to run cattle at Loco Man again," Wyatt confirmed, "but there's a lot to be done before we can stock up. I think I'll talk to this Pryor fellow to see if he knows what Dodd was up to."

"Rex Billings, he'll tell you how to find Pryor. He marry Billings' sister."

So, Pryor was Rex's brother-in-law. That was welcome news.

After Delgado left, Wyatt walked into the main house to find Tina scrubbing a huge cast-iron skillet. She blew a strand of hair out of her eyes and jerked her head at the old ice chest on the floor.

"If you're hungry, I made some sandwiches. There's fruit on the table and chips in the pantry."

"Sounds good. Thanks."

"The cooler has iced tea, too. I didn't sweeten it, but there's a sugar bowl next to the fruit bowl."

Wyatt didn't offer an opinion on that. Every real Texan knew that tea had to be sweetened while it was hot. He guessed they did things differently where Tina was from. After tasting the tea, though, he decided he could tolerate it unsweetened, as it was surprisingly mellow. He sat at the table and ate his lunch, pondering Dodd's actions and trying not to watch Tina as she vigorously scoured the heavy pan. Finally, she rinsed the skillet and transferred it to a flame on the stove, which flared considerably higher than the day before.

"Guess the propane delivery came," Wyatt said between bites of his ham sandwich.

She dried her hands with a towel, glancing at him. "It did."

"How bad was it?" he asked.

She pulled a folded piece of paper from the hip pocket of her jeans and showed it to him. He lifted his eyebrows and made an executive decision.

"We'll split the bill with you."

Tina blinked at that. "You will?"

"Seems to me we ought to be sharing all the utilities. And paying for groceries. At least so long as we're sharing the house."

"I'm not going to argue with that."

He bit his tongue to keep from blurting out how much that surprised him. Somehow he'd expected her to argue about every little thing, even when it worked to her advantage. Finishing his sandwich, he plucked an orange from the bowl on the table and sat back in his chair to peel it.

"Where are the boys?"

"Giving Ryder headaches, I imagine," she replied. "He was supposed to put Frankie down for a nap before patching the ceiling in that one bedroom. I told Tyler not to tag along with them, but Ryder said he didn't mind. Since Tyler and I are going to start his homeschooling tomorrow, I let it go."

Wyatt nodded, unconcerned but puzzled. Ryder was

good with Frankie. He didn't see why Ryder couldn't handle Tyler, too. On the other hand, he didn't understand why Tina didn't give the War Bonnet elementary school a chance. She had more than enough to do without adding homeschooling to the ever-growing list.

"I've always understood that the school here in War Bonnet is above average, with small classes, dedicated teachers and a solid curriculum. There was a time my folks thought about moving up here so my brothers and I could attend this school. If Dad's business hadn't taken off so well, I think they might've done it."

After his mom's death, his dad had almost sent him and his brothers here to live with Dodd. Wyatt would have welcomed that, but even at fifteen he'd understood that sending them away would have meant the end of Al Smith. Their dad had needed them as much as they'd needed him, so Wyatt had argued against the plan and promised to take on more responsibility than a fifteen-year-old ever should.

He wasn't certain that it had made any real difference in the end. It seemed to him that all Albert had ever done was go through the motions until he'd just given up. Sort of like Tina was doing right now. She pretended great interest in the condition of the worn wooden countertops, scrubbing them with a rag, though they already looked cleaner than Wyatt had ever seen them.

"Semester's already half-through," she said, industriously rubbing away with that limp rag.

"What difference does that make? At least Tyler would have a chance to make friends his own age."

"I know what's best for my own son," she snapped, whirling around to confront him.

Wyatt held up his hands in surrender. "I just wondered, that's all."

"Well, don't," she muttered, turning back to her task. At the last moment, she gave it up, tossing the rag into the sink.

Changing the subject, Wyatt asked, "Did Dodd say anything to you about planting grass?"

"Grass?" she echoed uncertainly. "Not that I recall. Why?"

Wyatt explained about the fenced fields of grass and the windmills. She shook her head.

"That doesn't make a bit of sense."

"Doesn't seem to, but Dodd usually knew what he was about."

She parked her hands on the edge of the counter behind her. "Like leaving you the land and me the house that sits on it?" she drawled sarcastically.

Maybe the old man had been losing it, after all. Wyatt pushed back his chair. "Think I'll head over to the Billings place and see if anyone there has a clue."

"Supper at six," Tina told Wyatt, as he made for the door, "and it's flashlights again tonight. Electrician can't come until tomorrow."

"At least there's hot water," he pointed out, pushing through the screen door, giving Tina one last surreptitious look before walking outside.

Why couldn't he seem to stop staring at the woman? He saw women every day who he barely noticed. Now the prickliest one he'd ever encountered, the one who'd messed up all his carefully designed plans, had him gawking like a teenage boy.

*Lord, whatever You're doing here*, he prayed silently as he strode for his truck, *I wish You'd let me in on it.*

God brought nothing to mind, however, as Wyatt drove toward Straight Arrow Ranch, so he supposed he'd just have to muddle through as best he could.

He caught Rex finishing up his lunch. His father, Wes, was there, along with the very fellow Wyatt most wanted to see.

Dean Pryor was a tall, muscular, fair-haired man with a ready smile. Wyatt could see why Delgado had referred to him as a boy. He had a sense of relaxed fun about him that was usually associated with carefree children. Still, no one could doubt Pryor's maturity or resist the sparkle of his blue eyes. Wyatt imagined that he was just the sort to charm every woman he met. He happily answered Wyatt's every question.

Unfortunately, Dean didn't have any idea why Dodd had hired him to sow grasses on the property, five varieties in all, especially as every site had been covered with natural grass already standing tall. The selections of sites and grasses had been well planned, however. Dodd had made sure that those varieties that most needed water had water available. The more drought-resistant varieties had gone in where no immediate water source was located.

"I thought he might be cooperating with a government test," Pryor reported, "but when I suggested that, he just about doubled over laughing."

"Did he explain why he fenced the grass fields?"

Pryor spread his broad, capable hands. "I didn't know he had."

No one else around the table seemed to have any answers for him.

"Boys, we better get back at it," Wes interjected before taking a final slug of his coffee. "I've got a list a mile long of things to get done before the wedding."

Wyatt glanced at Dean, though he definitely recalled Delgado saying that Pryor had already married Rex's sister. As if he knew what Wyatt was thinking, Dean grinned.

"Don't look at me. I'm married and got two kids already."

Everyone laughed. Wes raised his hand, saying, "I'm the groom. Y'all think you're so funny."

"Dad roped and tied the local doc," Rex chortled.

"Don't let Alice hear you say that," Callie scolded. "She'll rope, tie and sedate you."

"I'll be all for it by the time we get these calves cut," Rex declared, pushing up to his feet.

Dean, too, rose. "I might as well get back to playing cowboy before my wife comes looking for a babysitter."

"You picked a good day. It's Wednesday. We'll have to knock off early for prayer meeting tonight," said Wes.

"Stark might be able to pitch in," Rex suggested. "Why don't I give him a call?"

"Stark Burns is the busiest man I know," Wes said, shaking his head. "Even if that daughter of mine has slowed him down a notch or two."

"Wait," Wyatt interjected, pointing at Dean. "I thought he was married to your daughter."

"I've got two daughters," Wes said with a big grin. "Three, counting Callie here."

She went on tiptoe to kiss her father-in-law's cheek.

"If you need a hand, maybe I can help out," Wyatt volunteered.

"You know anything about cutting calves?" Rex asked.

"Not really," Wyatt admitted, "but I ought to, and I'm a fast learner."

"Can you ride and rope?" Wes asked.

"That I can do, but I might be a bit rusty."

"You're hired," Rex decreed. "We've got a bumper crop of bull calves this year, and the sooner we make 'em steers, the sooner they'll fatten up for market."

"I can call our ranch foreman, Delgado, to come over if you like."

"Now, why didn't we think of Delgado?" Rex asked.

The men all headed for the door, Wes joking, "I'm getting married soon. I've got enough on my mind. Why didn't *you* think of Delgado? You're the brains of the operation."

"Y'all heard him, boys," Rex bantered. "I am the official head of the Billings brain trust. Just remember that."

They were stomping into boots and reaching for hats in the foyer when Wyatt pulled out his cell phone to call Delgado. While he waited for the other man to answer, Rex glanced at the hat pegs on the wall, asking, "Where's your hat? You're gonna need it."

"Oh, I don't have one," Wyatt admitted, breaking off when Delgado finally answered. Wyatt explained the situation and heard the delight in his foreman's voice as he agreed to hurry over to the Billings ranch. "He's on his way," Wyatt announced, sliding the small phone back into his pocket. He looked up to find Wes and Rex standing with piles of battered cowboy hats in their hands.

"Let's try this one," Wes said, passing a stained, cream-colored hat to Wyatt.

After a moment, Wyatt realized he was meant to try on the hat. Unfortunately, it wobbled atop his head like a crown.

"Too small," Rex announced, plucking the hat off and pushing it into the bottom of his stack. "Maybe the straw." He plunked it onto Wyatt's head. Wyatt pushed it up out of his eyes.

"Too big," Wes decided. "Let's go with the old silver belly."

Tired and more than a bit floppy, the once handsome hat nestled down onto Wyatt's head as if made just for him.

"That's the one," Rex announced.

"It'll keep the sun from baking you, at least," Wes said, "but the satin lining's not exactly cool."

"Good thing it's not full summer yet," Dean put in, grinning as he pulled a baseball cap from his hip pocket and slung it onto his head.

"How come you get away with that?" Wyatt asked, only half teasing.

"Aw, I only wear cowboy hats to impress my wife," Dean said, "and that thing you're wearing would surely *not* do it."

They all walked out laughing, but Wyatt couldn't help thinking that a cowboy hat, even an old droopy one, surely made a man stand just a little prouder. As he strode along in the company of these men, Wyatt felt a surprising twinge of guilt at not calling to explain the situation to Tina. Then again, he decided, he hadn't promised to help repair the house. He was doing exactly what they'd agreed he'd do.

For some reason, he thought of her scrubbing that old skillet with such vigor. Then he pictured Callie Billings moving around her comfortable kitchen, and a pang of something like regret or disappointment struck him midchest. Ridiculous.

Tina Kemp was nothing like Rex's sweet wife. Her snappishness contrasted sharply with Callie's gentle admonitions. He suspected that Tina's silly ideas for opening a bed-and-breakfast in the Loco Man Ranch house were bound to end in failure, no matter how much he and his brothers tried to help, but maybe that was all part of God's plan. They'd have the house in good shape when she finally agreed to sell it to them. He'd have to ask Rex what a fair price might be. Later.

Or not.

## Chapter Five

$\sim\!\!\!\sim$

Wyatt dragged in to the house dusty and sweaty around five thirty that evening.

"I have never been so tired in my entire life."

Tina could believe it. He looked as if he'd been put through a meat grinder. She'd had a trying day herself. She'd climbed the stairs so many times today that her legs ached, but—between the shopping, cleaning and cooking—she'd managed to fix up Tyler's room and move her own things into the room with the missing window, which Ryder had temporarily boarded over. He'd carried in a bed from the bunkhouse for her, and she was already looking forward to sleep, so when Wyatt announced that he and his brothers were going to prayer meeting with the Billings family, she could only stare at him for several moments.

"Seriously?"

He nodded. "Don't know about you, but I've got plenty to be praying about."

"So do I," she admitted, "but I'll have to do my

praying here. I just don't have the energy to dress and go to church tonight."

"Your choice," Wyatt said lightly, glancing over the papers she'd left on the kitchen table. "What's this?"

"Utility transfer."

"I told you I'd take care of that," he reminded her, an edge to his voice.

"Yes, well, I had to drive into Ardmore to find everything Ryder needs, so I swung by the electric company. Turns out we don't have to worry about water and trash. We've got our own wells and have to haul our own trash."

"I think we can get trash pickup from the Town of War Bonnet if we want it."

"That would be great," she said. "I'm sure not up for hauling off my own trash."

"I'll check it out." Frowning at the papers, he said, "That's a big deposit for out here."

"Yeah, well, in Kansas City I rented an apartment with utilities included, so I don't have much of a record with the utility company." What records she did have, Layne's name was on the account as well as hers. She prayed they would not inform him for some reason. He was bound to find her eventually, but she hoped to be well established by then, with a presentable home for Tyler.

"I've got a lengthy track record with utility companies," Wyatt was saying. "I'll get over there and see if I can have this reduced."

"Don't bother," she snapped. "We can't even use the electricity. Besides, it's not your house."

He tossed his hands in the air. "I thought we agreed earlier today to split the utilities."

"Fine," she grumbled, knowing she was being unreasonable. The amount of the deposit, on top of the propane bill, had truly shocked her, and she was already fighting every moment of every day not to lose faith. Still, she didn't know why she had to take it out on him. Sucking in a deep breath, she calmed herself. "Having the account in both our names is the best thing. Thank you."

"No problem," he muttered. Then he added, "I'm hitting the shower."

"Water's hot," she told him, "but Ryder says the hot water heater will have to be replaced soon. The bottom is almost rusted out of this one."

Wyatt stared at her for a long moment before simply nodding and walking off.

Jake came in the door, sniffing. "Smells good. What's for supper?"

"Spaghetti with meat sauce."

Pipes squealed and banged, followed by the sound of water gushing.

"That Wyatt in there?"

"Yes."

"He tell you about prayer meeting?"

"I won't be going," she stated firmly. "Not tonight."

"Okay. Been a tough day, I take it."

She lifted the pot lid on the sauce. "You could say that, yeah."

"I'll wash my hands and set the table," he volunteered.

Shooting him a smile, she felt her mood lift ever so

slightly. Now, why didn't Wyatt's offers of help give her the same boost? Instead, everything he did irritated her in ways she couldn't even explain.

She opened cans of green beans, the salad she would have preferred being out of the question until they had refrigeration. So much seemed out of the question just now, even basic things like electricity. She wanted to sit down and have a good cry, but instead she turned back to the stove.

When Jake finished placing the plates, napkins and flatware, he went for glasses and filled them with ice from the ice chest before sitting the plastic jug of tea on the table.

"Hope Wyatt didn't insult your tea," Jake said conversationally. "He drinks what we call syrup tea, equal parts tea and sugar."

"The sugar's right there," Tina pointed out, waving a hand. "He can have all he wants."

Jake's eyes went wide. "You can't properly sweeten tea at the table. The sugar has to go in while the tea is boiling hot so it can dissolve as the tea steeps."

Tina waved an empty green-bean can at him. "Who says?"

"Texas." He chuckled at the expression on her face.

"For your information, Mr. Smith, at lunch your brother drank a full glass of my tea without a speck of sugar in it."

Jake feigned exaggerated shock, thumping himself in the chest. "My brother? Are you sure? He must be sweet on you if he drank your tea without sugar." Truly stunned by the mere suggestion that Wyatt might be sweet on her, Tina gaped at Jake. Stopping his teasing, Jake straightened. "It was just a joke."

"It wasn't funny."

Tina and Jake looked around to find Wyatt standing there wearing a clean white undershirt, his feet bare beneath the hems of his clean blue jeans.

"What smells so good?" Wyatt asked. Coming toward the table.

Tina whirled back to the stove.

Behind her, Jake said heartily, "Spaghetti. With meat sauce. And, uh, green beans, I think."

Walking a wide path around Wyatt and the table, Tina went into the foyer. At the foot of the staircase, she called loudly, "Supper!"

Tyler came running down the stairs. Ryder followed with Frankie perched on his shoulders. Tina saw at once that Frankie had managed to cover himself in the plaster Ryder had been using to mend the ceiling and cracks in the walls. She reached for the boy as Ryder stepped down onto the floor beside her. Frankie came into her arms easily, but he was so heavy that she nearly dropped him. Letting him slide down onto his feet, she dusted her hands and stepped back. Tyler seemed to have fared somewhat better, to her surprise. Still, his hands were covered with the stuff.

"Maybe I ought to hose you boys down before I put you in the tub." She glanced at Ryder, who wiped his dirty hands on his dirty shirt. Obviously, if he was going to prayer meeting with his brothers, he was going to have to clean up first. "Wash your hands and eat. Then, Ryder, you'd better clean up. I understand prayer meeting is on the agenda."

"Yeah?" He looked down at his hands and shrugged. "Okay."

"You clean up in the kitchen," she suggested. "I'll take the boys into the bathroom."

Nodding, Ryder went off to do as he was told. Not for the first time, Tina mused that he was a big, sweet-natured overgrown boy, whereas Wyatt... Wyatt Smith might be overbearing and assume he was in charge of the world, but he had no *boy* in him. He was all man.

By comparison, her ex, Layne, was urbane, polished, charming...selfish, spiteful to the point of brutality, deceptive. That was one thing she could say for Wyatt; he wasn't deceptive. When she got right down to it, the trait that so irked her about him was his arrogance.

She shepherded Tyler and Frankie down the hall to the bathroom. Once she had them as presentable as possible, Tina sent the boys to the kitchen. And she followed soon after.

Frankie sat atop the plastic tub again, while Tyler knelt on his chair seat.

"Sit on your bottom, son," she admonished gently as she went to put the finishing touches on the meal and carry it all to the table. He grumbled but complied. As she sat a steaming bowl of green beans in front of him, however, Tyler began to whine.

"I don't want that. I want spaghetti."

"We have spaghetti, but we need vegetables, too. Besides, you like green beans."

"Don't tell me what I like!" he shouted.

Tina recoiled at the familiar reprimand. It was something his father had said, often and hatefully. She'd put a dish on the table that Layne had previously praised only to find that he suddenly hated it. When she'd reminded him that he'd liked it before, he'd always snapped back just as Tyler had.

Momentarily stunned, Tina felt caught in the old quandary: Fight back or ignore it? From the corner of her eye, she caught Wyatt and Jake exchanging troubled glances. Her face heated, but she reminded herself that her six-year-old son was not his hateful father and she was the grown-up in this situation. As calmly as she could, she spooned green beans onto Tyler's plate and proceeded to do the same with the spaghetti.

"Eat," she ordered quietly.

Tyler frowned, but then he picked up his fork and dug into the spaghetti. Everyone else began filling their plates. Then they bowed their heads and Wyatt spoke the prayer.

"Father God, we thank You first for Your Son and then for all the many other blessings You've showered upon us. I thank You especially for new friends, this meal and the hands that prepared it. Amen."

Tina sent him a limp smile in acknowledgment for mentioning her—however obliquely—in his prayer, but she couldn't look him in the eye. She remembered the words that she'd thrown at him earlier.

*I know what's best for my own son.*

But did she really?

The meal rejuvenated Wyatt somewhat, but he still dragged along the edge of utter exhaustion. Yet he was eager to go to church. He wanted the comfort and assurance of prayer. Plus, he wanted to further his acquaintance with the Billings family and get to know the rest of his neighbors. He could learn a lot from Wes and Rex, and he couldn't have asked for more friendly company today. Besides, prayer meeting had to be better than sitting here in the dark house with Tina and her disrespectful son.

Wyatt was so used to correcting his brothers and nephew that he'd almost given Tyler a scolding when the boy had mouthed off at his mother. He had to give her points for remaining calm, though she obviously teetered on the edge of exhaustion herself. Still, if she didn't get control of that boy soon, she never would.

Wyatt didn't kid himself that his advice on the subject would be welcome, however. She'd made herself plain on the matter earlier.

*I know what's best for my own son.*

Wyatt kept his opinions to himself and concentrated on the food in front of him. It was simple but plentiful and tasty enough, especially considering that she was working without conveniences…like electricity. If she didn't get that fixed tomorrow, he'd see to it himself, though she was likely to tear a strip off his hide for it.

Having eaten his fill, he sat back and lifted the glass of tea that he hadn't yet touched.

"That was good. Thank you."

"You're welcome. I'll sweeten the next batch of tea while it's hot."

Wyatt glanced at her before taking a healthy swig of the tea. He let the cold tea slide down his throat before saying conversationally, "Actually, I like this. It's not at all bitter. What brand do you use?"

After a somewhat shocked silence, Tina named her preferred brand.

Ryder, who had demolished two plates of food to Wyatt's one, chugged his tea and reached for the plastic pitcher for a refill. "Wyatt's tea is like battery acid," he remarked easily. "Can't drink it without sugar."

"Hey!" Wyatt objected, much to Jake's amusement, though he couldn't deny the truth. "I never claimed to be a domestic whiz."

"You sure worry and fuss like someone's mother, though."

Wyatt rolled his eyes. "Just because I didn't want you to fight—" Too late, he broke off, grimacing and tilting his head in apology to Ryder.

Tina flashed a glance around the table. "I wouldn't want Tyler to join the military, either," she said, assuming the most obvious interpretation of Wyatt's comment. Then her eyes widened, and she addressed herself to Jake. "That is, unless he truly wanted a military career. It is a noble profession. I just wouldn't want him in harm's way."

Jake smiled warmly and ran his fingertip around the rim of his tea glass. "I didn't exactly give our mother hen over here the opportunity to talk me out of enlisting."

"You didn't," Wyatt accused, relieved to have the conversation channeled in this direction. He looked at Tina, lifted an eyebrow and said, "He joined the day after his eighteenth birthday. Reported for basic training within weeks of graduating high school."

"One of the best decisions I ever made. Served over ten years."

"But then you got out before you reached retirement age," Tina prodded gently.

Jake looked down, licking his lips. "I took a hardship release when my wife passed away."

Tina grimaced. "I'm so sorry. I didn't realize."

Jake shrugged. "She was military, too. You have to expect it when you marry a soldier. Training exercise."

Tina pulled in a deep breath. "I'm very sorry for your loss."

"She was doing what she loved," Jake said softly. "That's what I try to remember."

Tina merely offered him a small smile.

Again, irritation swamped Wyatt. He didn't like the feeling, and he didn't even want to know why. He couldn't be jealous of his own brother. Could he? Certainly not over Tina. He didn't even like her. Except… he wasn't sure anymore what it was about her that he disliked so much. He cleared his throat.

"I don't want to be late for prayer meeting."

Ryder finished his second glass of tea and plunked the tumbler onto the table. "I need to clean up."

"Well, don't take all night," Jake called after him. "I've still got to get Frankie cleaned up."

"Why don't you let Frankie stay here with Tyler and me?" Tina suggested, smiling at Jake again.

That smile rankled Wyatt. The two of them seemed to be getting along like a house on fire. She could barely be civil to Wyatt, but she was all smiles for Jake. The thought made Wyatt cringe. Oh, yeah. A good night for prayer meeting.

"I don't want you to have to bathe him tonight," Jake

was saying, waving a hand at Frankie. "He's filthy, and you're tired."

"I've got to bathe Tyler anyway."

"I can wash myself," Tyler objected loudly.

Tina smiled stiffly at Jake. "There. Tyler can wash himself, so I'm free to take care of Frankie."

Tyler opened his mouth, but Wyatt cut him off, fed up with mouthy kids and this Tina-Jake thing. "I guess y'all want to turn in early since you start Tyler's classes tomorrow."

"What classes?" Tyler demanded, frowning.

"Schoolwork," Tina replied lightly. "We don't want you to fall behind in your studies."

"They have a good school here in town," Jake pointed out.

"I told her that."

"I made a thorough check before I agreed to this move," Jake went on.

Suddenly, Tyler gripped the edge of the table in front of him and shouted, "I want to go to my old school! I want to go home!"

Visibly blanching, Tina tried to placate him. "Son, we are home. And tonight you can sleep in your own room. It has all your toys and books in it and the same blanket and pillows. Your stuffed fox is there, and—"

Tyler leapt to his feet, bawling at her. "It's not my room! That's stupid! *You're* stupid!"

"Whoa," Wyatt said, at the very end of his patience, but Tyler was already running down the hallway.

Obviously embarrassed, Tina quickly rose to follow her son, but first she apologized for him. "I'm sorry for that. He's unsettled and confused and…" Her explanation dwindled away.

"He called you stupid," Wyatt pointed out. "You can't let him get away with that."

Her chin came up but not her gaze. "He's just repeating what he heard his father say so often."

Wyatt's stomach churned. No wonder she was prickly. He softened his tone. "All the more reason to put a stop to it. People shouldn't speak to each other that way. Males especially shouldn't speak that way to females. He has to learn that."

She nodded and turned away, softly saying, "I'll clean this up later."

"We'll handle this," Wyatt told her. "You go talk to your boy."

"I'll take Frankie into the shower with me," Jake decided aloud, "and get him ready for bed."

"Thank you," she replied in a choked voice. Then she followed Tyler from the room.

When she was gone, Jake pointed a finger at Frankie. "I don't ever want to hear you say anything so disrespectful to any adult." Big-eyed, Frankie nodded, and Jake immediately softened. "I know you won't. Hopefully, in time, Tyler will learn not to misbehave like that, too."

"Hopefully," Wyatt muttered, but with a father who called his mother names in front of him, the kid already had a strike against him. Wyatt felt a new empathy for both Tina and Tyler.

Oh, yeah. Tonight was a really good night for prayer meeting.

## Chapter Six

Apparently, showing up for prayer meeting at the Countryside Church was tantamount to announcing to the community at large that the Smith brothers were in residence. The first to mention it was the electrician recommended by the Billings family, who stopped by the next day.

"Everyone's excited to have y'all at Loco Man Ranch," the thin, fortyish man said to Tina. "Wouldn't be the same without a Smith here, and now there's five or six of you."

"Three," Tina corrected. "That is, four: Wyatt, Jake, Ryder and little Frankie."

"Oh, you're not a member of the family?"

"Uh, not exactly." She didn't want to go into details, so she said simply, "Dodd was my stepfather."

That raised his shaggy eyebrows, so she quickly turned the conversation to business. After describing the problems, she wasn't surprised to hear that the entire house would need rewiring, and while the price of the project was not as much as she'd feared, she still broached the subject of providing the materials herself. The electrical contractor proved amenable, so she took out her cell phone and turned it on. She had been careful to keep it off for fear that Layne would try to track her through it, but she needed to call the wholesaler.

Thankfully, the conversation was brief. It took the electrician longer to write out a detailed list than it did for the wholesaler to agree to provide the materials at wholesale.

After some finagling, the electrical contractor left to get the supplies, promising Tina they would have power in at least part of the house by nightfall.

As soon as the electrician departed, guests began arriving. A battered pickup arrived, containing three women, one of them a mere teenager who couldn't have graduated high school even a year earlier. They brought with them a cake in a foil pan.

"Mrs. Smith?"

"I'm Tina Kemp, Dodd's stepdaughter. There is no Mrs. Smith."

"Well, that's good news," declared one of the women, a willowy blonde with sharp features and entirely too much makeup.

Tina was shocked into silence as the elder of the women introduced herself as Sharon Umber. Sharon introduced her daughters, Peggy and Olive.

"We met the Smith brothers at church last night," Peggy gushed.

"And of course we want to welcome them to War Bonnet," said her mother. "Uh, I mean, we want to welcome all of you." With that, she pushed the pan at Tina. "Chocolate cake."

"Thank you," Tina managed to say, inviting them to sit at the kitchen table with a wave of her hand.

While she filled glasses with iced tea, Peggy asked, "Are the Smith brothers here?"

"Jake's around here somewhere," Tina said. "Ryder's upstairs working. I'm not sure where Wyatt is, but he's on ranch business, I'm sure."

"And you're what? The housekeeper here?" Mrs. Umber wanted to know.

"I'm the homeowner," Tina stated flatly. "Dodd left the ranch to his nephews and the house to me. They're only staying here temporarily."

Sharon Umber looked confused, but then she glanced around the old-fashioned, bare-bones kitchen and remarked, "I imagine someone will be building a new house soon, then."

"Well, it won't be me," Tina said. "I like this house, and I intend to refurbish it."

"There's sure nothing around here to rent," Mrs. Umber said. "I hear Lyons is building apartments, though."

"A rancher doesn't want to live in an apartment." Her youngest daughter scoffed. "Especially if he's got a wife."

"Better and better!" declared Peggy, giggling.

Tina almost choked on her polite laughter. No doubt Sharon and her daughters were calculating which of the brothers was most likely to build that new house and just how likely he needed a wife. Tyler and Frankie ran into the room just then, asking for a snack.

Tina cleared her throat. "How does chocolate cake sound?"

The boys bounced up and down, yelling, "Yay!"

Tina parked them at the table, introducing each to the Umbers, and went for paper plates and the milk carton. She was still dishing out cake when another vehicle arrived, with two women this time: Mrs. Carla Landis and her friend Marti Jewel, a single woman in her thirties. They brought cookies. Tina made room at the table and went for more glasses. When the third car showed up, the Umbers finally excused themselves.

Meri Billings Burns and her sister, Ann Billings Pryor, brought flour, sugar, canned vegetables and homemade jams, which would come in very handy. Moreover, they were there to see Tina rather than check out the trio of bachelor brothers. Meri showed photos of her baby girl. Ann, too, had a daughter, a toddler, as well as a son in first grade.

"We'll have to get Donovan and these boys together soon," Ann said, smiling at Frankie and Tyler.

"That would be wonderful," Tina said. "Tyler could use a friend closer to his age."

"We'll make it happen," Ann promised. "And I'll have Donovan look for Tyler at school. I hope we can expect to see you both on Sunday as it's Easter."

"Easter," Tina echoed uncertainly. She'd forgotten all about it. She'd always made a big deal of Easter with Tyler, and this year she hadn't even thought of it.

"Yes, we'll be at Easter services," she promised, returning to the table, "but Tyler won't be attending public school."

"Why ever not?" Carla Landis wanted to know. "My sister and brother-in-law both teach there. It's an excellent school."

"I—I just think Tyler is…safer at home for now."

Carla and her friend Marti immediately said they had to leave. Fearing she had offended them, Tina thanked them for coming as she walked them to the door. Turning back to the Billings sisters, she sighed.

"I didn't handle that very well."

"Oh, don't worry about Carla," Meri said. "She's thin skinned, but she gets over it quickly."

"I hope you'll reconsider sending Tyler to public school, though," Ann added.

Tina shook her head. "I can't. I just…can't."

The sisters smiled and changed the subject. Tina again promised that she and Tyler would be in church on Sunday. The women made approving sounds before getting to their feet.

"I need to start Stark's lunch," Meri said.

"And we really should rescue Callie," Ann put in. "She's got her kids and ours today."

"Thank you so much for coming by," Tina said, ushering them to the door, "and please give Callie my best."

The sisters took their leave. Sighing with mingled relief and pleasure—Meri and Ann were two women she felt she could truly be friends with—Tina turned back to the table, only to spy Ryder standing there with his arms folded.

"You hiding from someone, Tina?"

"What? Don't be silly." Flustered, she forced herself to walk calmly across the room to begin clearing the table. "Why would you ask such a thing?"

He looked at her for a long moment; then he dropped

his hands to his waist. "Takes one to know one, I guess," he muttered, turning away.

She wanted to call him back, ask what he meant by that, but she didn't dare. A woman who couldn't bear questions couldn't ask them, either. She just couldn't chance that one of the brothers would decide she was unfairly keeping her son from Layne and notify him.

Recalling what Meri had said about making her husband's lunch, Tina started building sandwiches. Wrapping them, she stowed them in the cooler before slicing an apple and rinsing the slices in pineapple juice to keep them from browning. She'd serve the remaining juice to the boys with their supper. All the while, she pondered her situation.

Could she really operate this decrepit house as a B and B? She looked at the old refrigerator. It wasn't nearly large enough, but until it was running again, she dared not open any of the jars that the Billings sisters had brought with them or even stock the larder sufficiently.

For the sake of her son, she would somehow make this work. She knew in her heart of hearts that Layne would destroy the child out of sheer maliciousness if he ever gained full custody. He'd turn Tyler into a hateful, belligerent younger version of himself just to hurt her.

So, yes, she would hide, and she would homeschool, and she would spend every penny she had to keep Tyler from his father.

And she would pray.

For all the good that seemed to do.

* * *

"You sure you're not letting your own situation color your judgment?" Wyatt asked softly, dropping down next to his brother on the porch step two evenings later.

Ryder shook his head, his gaze focused on his hands. Apparently, he'd deliberated quite a while before telling Wyatt what he'd overheard.

Ryder and Tina had made real progress over the past few days. The place was clean and organized. The porch was sound and the ceiling patched. Wallpaper had been stripped away in the dining room and new drapes hung. Nearly the whole house had been re-wired, so they had lights, refrigeration and hot water out of the faucet. Wyatt was looking forward to a little TV tonight, but he'd returned from visiting area cattle breeders to find Ryder hanging around outside, waiting for him.

"If she's not hiding, why won't she let that boy go to school?" Ryder wanted to know. "And why does she keep her phone turned off? The electrician complained about it, said he normally calls his clients if he needs something while he's working, but with her, he has to stop what he's doing and go in search of her because she keeps her phone off."

Wyatt frowned. "Maybe she just doesn't want to run down the battery. When you asked her, she denied that she was hiding. Right?"

"Yeah," Ryder admitted. "Sort of. I'd have let it go after that if not for what the electrician told me. And there's something else."

"What's that?"

"Tyler asked me to call his dad and tell him where they are."

Wyatt grimaced. "Man, I do not want to get in the middle of that."

"I understand," Ryder said, "but if she's hiding Tyler from his father…"

Wyatt shook his head. "We don't know that. But I'll talk to her after supper, see what I can find out."

Ryder nodded. "I hate to be the one to bring this up, considering my own situation."

"You're hiding from the press, not a legal situation."

"Still, if anybody knows there are good reasons to hide, I do."

Sighing, Wyatt clapped his baby brother on the shoulder. Would he ever recover from the tragedy? Accidentally killing his sparring partner in practice had nearly broken Ryder.

Then Uncle Dodd had died and left them the ranch. The solution had fallen straight into Wyatt's lap, and he was still convinced that it was the right move, despite the complication of Tina.

So far, Wyatt had dealt with her by having as little to do with her as possible. That didn't keep him from thinking about her, though. Her beauty seemed to blossom more fully every day, particularly as he came to see a softer side to her. She was more vulnerable than she wanted anyone to know, especially when it came to her son, which meant that Wyatt couldn't put off this conversation.

After a supper that included an excellent meatloaf, he made sure that Jake got the boys ready for bed while he helped Tina clean the kitchen. He meant to take her into the den for a private conversation, but no sooner had she folded the last dish towel than she pushed open the screen door and walked down the steps out into the night. Wyatt followed, closing the back door behind him.

She turned, arms crossed, when she heard the door close, then she turned away again. "I could never get enough of the stars. They're always so bright out here. Dodd and I used to sit on the front porch steps and gaze up at the night sky while Mom watched one of her silly shows. Having the old TV working again made me think of those nights. People in the city don't even realize how many stars there are."

"That's true," Wyatt said. "The night sky in Houston is a murky gray with a few dim twinkles." He waited, sliding his hands into the pockets of his jeans, but she didn't say anything else, so he took the bull by the horns. "Tina, we need to talk."

She glanced over her shoulder, her eyes gleaming in the moonlight. "What about?"

"Are you hiding from someone or something?"

Looking away, she hugged herself a little tighter. "Ryder asked me that earlier, and I can't imagine why either of you would think such a thing."

Wyatt noticed that she hadn't exactly denied the accusation. "Would you tell me if you were?"

"That would be foolish, wouldn't it?"

Disappointed, Wyatt bowed his head, sending up a quick prayer for the right words. "It's starting to look like you're hiding Tyler from his father."

Gasping, she whirled around. "Why would you say such a thing?"

He heard the tremor in her voice and sighed. "Tina, if he has custody of Tyler—"

"I have custody of Tyler," she interrupted hotly. "Full custody granted by a court," she added. "But Layne is threatening to sue for custody. His lawyers advised me b-before I left Kansas."

Wyatt rubbed his hands over his face, suddenly quite tired. "I see. So, this is your way of avoiding a custody battle you fear you'll lose."

Tina rushed forward into the rectangle of light thrown onto the ground from the window in the door behind and above Wyatt. He caught his breath. She was the most amazingly beautiful woman he'd ever seen, but he couldn't let that sway him. He had to know the truth.

"You don't understand," she said. "Layne's parents have money, lots of it. They've never been particularly interested in being grandparents...or parents, so far as I can tell, but their usual way of dealing with Layne is to simply give him what he wants. Art school in Paris. A lavish wedding. A house. Cars."

"So, he basically has unlimited funds to fight you in court."

"Yes."

"Why didn't he do it at the time of the divorce then?"

"Tyler was too small, too much trouble, I imagine. He and Layne simply weren't that close, but as Tyler has gotten older, Layne's tried to influence him. He pushes Tyler to pick sides between us, and he courts him with expensive gifts and entertainment. He tells Tyler lies about our marriage, and he knows I won't tell him the truth because it's not good for Tyler to know that I caught Layne cheating on me."

Wyatt could hardly imagine such a thing. Why would a man cheat on a woman like Tina? Wyatt rubbed the nape of his neck.

"I'm sorry you had to go through that, but I have to ask if you're allowed to take Tyler out of state without his dad's permission."

"Yes. But that won't keep Layne from filing for custody. He claims that I can't provide adequately for Tyler and that I don't spend enough time with him. He's even tried to say that I've alienated Tyler's affections, though it's Layne who's tried to do that. I never criticize him to Tyler, because it's not good for Tyler to hear awful things about his dad." She shoved her fingers into her hair, adding, "He'll eventually figure it out on his own, anyway. Unless Layne warps him, which he would do just to spite me." She flailed her arms in a gesture of exasperation.

Wyatt tucked his hands back into the pockets of his jeans to keep from reaching out and pulling her into his embrace.

"Like you said, Tyler will eventually figure it out."

"If he has the chance," she qualified. "I'd hoped this move would bring us closer together. I don't intend to keep him away from his father. I just want a chance to build a closer relationship with him myself."

"The B and B is a way for you to spend more time with him, isn't it?" Wyatt realized suddenly.

She nodded. "I'd hoped he'd love it here as much as I do," she said in a small voice. "I think eventually he will. If he spends enough time here."

"Makes sense," Wyatt admitted, though he was far from comfortable with the situation.

"What scares me most—" she went on in a voice barely above a whisper "—is to what lengths Layne would go to hurt me through Tyler. I—I really believe he's too lazy and self-involved to actually…" She blinked back tears. "To *physically* hurt Tyler."

Chilled by the prospect, Wyatt hurried to reassure her. "Surely not. He'd have to be psychotic to actually harm his own son."

"Right." She tried a smile, but it was wan and fleeting. "It's just that…I'm not sure Layne is truly capable of loving anyone other than himself, Tyler included."

Rocked, Wyatt said, "We'll certainly pray that those fears are unfounded, and in the meantime you're both safe here."

"Yes," she said, sounding as if she was trying to convince herself. "This is the safest place for us."

"Well, thanks for telling me what's going on."

She nodded. "I—I was afraid to before. Afraid you'd insist on telling Layne where we are."

"No, I won't do that. Not at this point. But you should know that Tyler has asked Ryder to call his dad."

Shaking her head, she clapped a hand over her mouth. Several seconds ticked by before she dropped her hand and whispered, "Thank you."

"You don't have to thank me," he told her.

"Actually," she said, "you've been pretty good about everything. You and your brothers."

Wyatt grimaced, knowing he hadn't been very nice in the beginning. "It was the shock at first," he admitted. "And, well, I can't let anything interfere with our plans."

"I understand."

"You don't, really," he said, bowing his head. What could he do except tell her then? "It's Ryder." He explained the situation, how Ryder had accidentally killed a young man while practicing for a cage fight. "It almost destroyed him, and he still carries a huge burden of guilt, though he and the trainer were both cleared, even of the negligence charge. That didn't keep the press from hounding them mercilessly, though. I had to get him out of Houston."

"Oh, no," she said. "That's heartbreaking. Ryder's so patient and gentle with the kids. I can't imagine him as a fighter."

"Mixed martial arts was a fitness thing with him. But he has skills, and people noticed. Before I knew it, he'd signed a contract to compete in the MMA circuit. He won his first two matches. Then Bryan died in a freak accident... I thought we were going to have to bury Ryder, too."

"I'm so sorry."

"I'd appreciate it if you wouldn't say anything to him."

"I won't."

"We'll make this work for everyone," Wyatt promised. "Listen, do you mind if I speak to Tyler? I'd like him to know that he can come to me or my brothers with any questions or problems."

She pondered that, then nodded. "If you need me, I'll be sitting on the front porch."

He smiled and turned toward the steps, silently praying for wisdom, discernment and the strength to avoid the temptation of Tina's beauty.

The last thing either of them needed at this point was another complication.

No matter how lovely that complication might be.

## Chapter Seven

W yatt tapped on Tyler's bedroom door before opening it. The boy lay atop his narrow bed, a book in his hands.

"What's that?" Wyatt asked lightly. "Bedtime story?"

Tyler nodded and turned a page, letting Wyatt know that this interruption was unwelcome. Wyatt let him know that he wasn't going away by coming fully into the room.

"Has your mom read that to you?" Wyatt asked, but Tyler shook his head.

"I read it myself."

"Not many six-year-olds can read books all by themselves."

Tyler dropped a finger onto the page and read aloud, "Look at the baby bird. It has no...no...feats...feats her."

"Feathers," Wyatt corrected. "It has no feathers. That's very good, Ty."

The boy frowned over the top of his book. "That's not my name."

Wyatt smiled. "It's a nickname, a shortened version of your whole name. You know, Frankie is a nickname, too. I suppose someday he'll outgrow Frankie and we'll start calling him Frank, but his real name is Francis."

Tyler dropped his book onto his lap. "What kind of name is that? I didn't hear that name before."

"Francis is one of those names that can be used for a girl or a boy, depending on how it's spelled. Frankie is named after my mom, his grandmother."

Tyler sat up in the bed. "I wouldn't want to be named after no girl."

Wyatt shrugged. "It's our way of honoring our mom. She was great, and we loved her."

"I'd hate to be named after my mom."

Chuckling, Wyatt said, "Yeah, that wouldn't work too well. There's no boy equivalent of Tina. What's her middle name?"

"Lynette."

"Guess she could have named you Tyler Lynn."

He shook his head. "I'm Tyler Walker Kemp."

"Walker is your mom's maiden name, so you are named after her."

Tyler's mouth dropped open. Obviously, he'd never made the connection. "I don't want to be named after her! She's stupid!"

Shocked, Wyatt had to work to keep his cool. "Your mother is not stupid."

"She is! My dad says so."

White-hot anger flashed through Wyatt, but he tamped it down. "Real men don't call women stupid, Tyler."

"Even if they are?" the boy shot back.

"Your mother is an extremely intelligent woman," Wyatt stated, "and I don't ever want to hear you say she's stupid again. She's brilliant and obviously talented. Just look at what she's done with this room."

Tyler glanced around, clearly puzzled. Three of the walls had been painted a rich, deep blue. The fourth had been painted a restful green to match his bedspread, which was covered with colorful race cars. On the green wall, she'd hung an old mirror, the simple frame of which she'd painted yellow to match the chest of drawers beneath it. On either side of the mirror, she'd hung yellow-and-white checked flags. Car posters had been placed strategically around the room, on the yellow closet door, at the head of the yellow-painted bed, on the ceiling above it and over a short set of yellow shelves filled with books and toys. All in all, she'd done an amazing job with nothing more than a couple of cans of paint.

"What's more, yours is the only room in the house that's finished," Wyatt went on. "She put you first. She always puts you first."

Frowning, Tyler picked at his bedspread. "If she's so smart, how come she was such a bad wife my dad had to divorce her?"

Wyatt had to think about how to answer that. He couldn't break Tina's confidence about how her marriage had ended, but he couldn't let Tyler go on believing the divorce was Tina's fault. Walking over to the bed, he sat on the end and fixed Tyler with a blunt look.

"It takes two people to make a marriage work, Tyler, and it takes two people to destroy one."

"He wouldn't of cheated on her with that other woman if she'd been a better wife," Tyler shot back.

Wyatt felt his jaw drop. "Your father told you about that?"

Tyler nodded. Wyatt couldn't tell if he was confused or ashamed. Maybe both.

"He had no business telling you that," Wyatt stated evenly. "Do you even know what *cheating* means?"

Sullenly, Tyler shrugged. Somewhat relieved, Wyatt chose his next words carefully.

"Your mom could have told you about your dad's cheating, but she didn't want to make him look bad. She wants you to love and respect your father. Whatever he says, their divorce was not your mother's fault, certainly not hers alone. Someday you'll understand that. Meanwhile, I hope you're big enough, smart enough and brave enough to trust that your parents' divorce has nothing to do with you. They both love you. You need to leave it at that. And so does your father."

"He says he's gonna run her out of money and take me to live with him," Tyler revealed, sounding worried. "And then I won't see her no more."

Obviously, Tina had been right about everything. To tell his young son about his cheating and blame Tina for it was the act of a selfish, egotistical individual. Obviously, Layne Kemp wasn't fit to be a father, but Wyatt wouldn't say so to the boy.

"Your mother will never let that happen," Wyatt assured Tyler. "You're the most important person in the world to her. She made this move to Oklahoma so she can spend more time with you and give you a great life. You need to stop giving her a hard time about it.

And when you see your father again, I hope you'll let him know that you want to spend time with both him and your mother. You do, don't you?"

"Yes," Tyler whispered.

"Good," Wyatt said, standing up, then leaning over to help ease Tyler down onto his pillow. "I'm glad to hear that. And if you ever need to talk about stuff, Ty, you can always come to me. Or my brothers. Okay?"

"Okay, Wyatt," Tyler said.

Wyatt ruffled the boy's reddish blond hair, pleased to get a grin out of him. Then he tucked the covers around him and said good-night before slipping from the room. Unfortunately, now he had to tell Tina what Tyler had revealed.

Hearing the door open at her back, Tina inwardly sighed. She'd been arguing with herself about the wisdom of letting Wyatt talk to her son in private. On one hand, Wyatt had a right to check her story, which he was no doubt doing. On the other, she could never be sure anymore how Tyler would react. She had no secrets now, so she didn't worry that he would expose her, but she could only hope that he wouldn't make an enemy of Wyatt.

Wyatt walked across the porch and sat down on the top step beside her. The night breeze swirled his scent around her, an earthy smell, part grass, part wood and part male. Her heart skipped a beat. She closed her eyes, focusing on thoughts of her son.

"Did you find out what you needed to know?"

"We established that I can call him Ty from now on." That surprised her, and she looked around, eyebrows raised. "The rest of us have nicknames. Everyone but you."

She relaxed. "Unless you count Mom as a nickname."

"There is that," Wyatt agreed with a smile, but then he sobered. "I'm afraid you're right about everything you said about your ex. He told Tyler that he cheated on you."

She gasped. "He *told* Tyler?"

Wyatt took her hand in his, nodding. "But he told Tyler it was your fault for being such a bad wife."

"Oh, that's so like Layne!" she exploded bitterly. "He doesn't care that he's burdened his son with information that he's too young to understand. All he cares about is vindicating himself and hurting me."

No wonder Tyler was acting out. He had to be so confused and angry. She'd tried to protect him from the truth of his father's infidelity, and all along Layne had been feeding him a warped version of what had happened. Her poor boy. Suddenly, it was all too much. She burst into tears.

Long, strong arms came around her from the side. "Please don't cry."

"I'm s-sorry," she stuttered, scrubbing at the tears.

"No apology necessary," he crooned, brushing back her bangs. "You didn't tell your son things he shouldn't know, and you've read your ex correctly. Take comfort in that. Ty says he's filed for custody in an effort to bankrupt you, so now we can plan accordingly."

*We.* Even as she told herself how foolish it would be to take Wyatt literally, that one tiny word comforted her. She gulped down the remainder of her tears.

"I thought he was my white knight," she went on. "He asked me to marry him the day after my mother's funeral. I felt rescued and grateful. I thought he loved me."

"I'm sure he did," Wyatt said softly, "as much as he was able."

"He isn't able. It wasn't long before I realized that I'd married the male equivalent of my mother." She straightened, breaking contact with him. "Layne refused to split anything, and because his parents' names were on the deed to the house, he didn't have to let me back inside, so all I had was what I left with. Thankfully, I never added him to my car title, or I wouldn't even have transportation."

"Layne didn't even provide for his son?"

"He agreed to child support, but he hid most of his income. By the time he finally signed the papers, all I wanted was to be free of him. And custody of my son."

"Sounds like you had your priorities right."

"Doesn't matter. I always vowed I'd never get divorced. I don't want to be like my mother. She was married five times."

"Whoa. That had to be tough for you."

"It was. She couldn't be alone but she couldn't be in love, either. Until my marriage busted up, I never realized how hard being alone could be."

"You'll find the right man."

"No," Tina said, "I won't. I haven't dated since the divorce. And I don't intend to."

He seemed surprised. "Don't you ever want to marry again?"

She shook her head. "How could I be sure it wouldn't turn out like the first time?"

"You have to trust yourself. You have to believe you won't make the same mistake twice."

"But I can't believe that," she countered. "My mother is proof that you can make the same mistake repeatedly."

"You can, but you don't have to, especially if you pray about the matter."

She rolled her eyes. "Do you think I haven't prayed about this? For so long I believed that no self-respecting man would want me. When Layne showed interest, I thanked God. But I was just fooling myself."

"How could you possibly believe that no man would want you?"

She lifted her shoulders, muttering, "My mother was very beautiful."

"So are you."

She stared at him skeptically. Suddenly, everything changed. Her heartbeat stuttered to a stop. She held her breath, watching as he fought the urge to kiss her. Part of her hoped he would, if only to prove that she was desirable, lovable; part of her wanted to bolt, in case that kiss proved to her just how truly vulnerable she was. She didn't move so much as an eyelash.

After a long moment rife with tension, he leaned back slightly and shifted his gaze. Unexpected disappointment crashed through Tina, but she had lots of experience in keeping a placid, enigmatic expression.

"Listen," he said, "don't worry. I'll talk to Jake and Ryder, make sure they understand the situation. They don't need all the details, but I promise they'll agree with me. You and Ty are safe here."

Tina stared up at the night sky. "I can't tell you how much I appreciate your understanding."

"I'm just glad you told me," he said softly. "I wouldn't have wanted to unintentionally put you or Tyler at risk."

He pushed up to his feet then. Keeping her seat, she looked up at him. Oh, how she wished he was not so disturbingly attractive. That coupled with his kindness and his strength made him very nearly irresistible. It was the last thing she needed right now.

She hadn't counted on wanting Wyatt Smith's support, his understanding, his advice, his faith. Him.

Maybe she was more like her mother than she even knew. All the more reason to focus entirely on her son.

After Wyatt left, she went upstairs to check on Tyler. He was sound asleep, so she kissed his forehead and tiptoed from the room.

The next morning, she greeted him with great good cheer. "Happy Easter!"

Nothing was said of his discussion with Wyatt the night before. Tyler seemed pleasant enough initially, but the situation quickly deteriorated into all-out rebellion.

He didn't like the clothes she'd laid out for him to wear to church. He didn't like his breakfast, though any other day he'd have begged for cold cereal. He didn't like the idea of going into a Bible class of strangers, even if they were his own age. And he really, really did not want to ride to church with Tina.

"I want to ride with Frankie!" Tyler insisted for the umpteenth time, refusing to get into her car.

Tina dug deep within for patience. "We don't have time for this."

"Tell you what," Jake said, coming through the back door and setting Frankie onto his feet. "We'll get you a second safety seat for Wyatt's truck. That way we won't have to take the time to move the seat. That's what we've done for Frankie. When we get the extra safety seat for Wyatt's truck, you can ride with Frankie. But for today, you ride with your mom. Deal?"

In reply, Tyler folded his arms and tucked his chin stubbornly.

"No? Sorry. I don't think you have any other options this morning."

"You're not the boss of me!" Tyler bawled at Jake.

Tina felt her face flood with color and immediately took her son by the arm, bending close to whisper, "Stop this. Right now."

She felt Wyatt step up beside her. "You may not like what Jake has to say, Ty, but I am the boss of the whole Loco Man Ranch, so you *will* listen to me." He didn't shout, but he didn't leave any wiggle room, either. "It's time we laid down some rules. One, the children on the Loco Man will not speak to adults with disrespect. That goes for your mom, Jake, me, Ryder, Delgado and any other adult who comes on the place. It means no shouting, ugly names or insults. And no stomping feet. Got it?"

For a long moment Tyler did not respond, but then he nodded sullenly. Tina sent an apologetic glance at Wyatt, who continued speaking.

"Second, it's fine for you to ask for what you want. You can even argue for it. But shouting is out. If you can't make your point without shouting, then you don't have a good point to make. The moment you start shouting, you've lost the argument. Understand?"

Tyler's chin trembled, and he started to cry, wailing brokenly, "I wanna go home."

Tina slid her arm across his shoulders. "Sweetie, I keep telling you that we are home. I know you don't like the house much right now, but in time we'll have it all fixed up. You'll see. Besides, our old apartment has been rented to someone else by now." That made him turn his face into her body and sob all the harder. "Oh, Tyler," she crooned, "if you just give Loco Man Ranch a chance, I know you'll come to like it here. And listen, we're going to color eggs and hunt for them later."

As she spoke, Frankie walked over to Tyler and patted him. "S'okay."

Tyler shrugged off his hand. "You like it here 'cause you got your dad."

Tina traded concerned looks with Wyatt, who said, "You'll see your dad before long."

"I don't never see him," Tyler grumbled.

"You know that's not true," Tina countered.

"Not as much as I want."

She couldn't argue with that. Even in Kansas City, Layne hadn't taken full advantage of the many opportunities to see his son, and when he had, Tyler had come home even unhappier than before. Frankie patted Tyler again, pointing to Wyatt with his free hand.

"Unca Wyatt be your daddy," he said, as if offering Tyler a prized toy.

Tina's jaw dropped, and when she looked at Wyatt, his hung agape, too. Ryder and Jake laughed behind their hands.

Her face burning hot, Tina ignored Frankie's gesture and tried to reassure her son. "You'll see your dad as soon as the B and B is operational. If not before. I promise."

To her surprise, Tyler started drying his eyes.

"We'd better go. Don't want to be late on Easter Sunday," Wyatt muttered, heading toward his truck. Jake took Frankie by the hand, drawing him along with him as he followed Wyatt, Ryder falling into step beside them. He and Ryder still chuckled and whispered together.

Tina quickly turned to open the back door of her car for Tyler. He climbed up into his seat without argument, and she smiled her appreciation as she buckled his belt.

All the while, she couldn't help thinking that Wyatt would be an excellent father, far better for her son than Layne. But then, so would all the Smith brothers. Not that she would ever consider marrying any of them.

Still, she remembered the way Wyatt had looked at her the night before. She couldn't suppress feelings and emotions that she hadn't felt in years.

# Chapter Eight

"We could make a morning of it," Ann Pryor said, smiling at Tina as they stood in the foyer of the church after the service. Wyatt listened with unabashed interest. "Bring Tyler and Frankie," Ann went on. "You and I can get to know each other better, and the boys can play. Dean's grandmother will want to make lunch for us, I'm sure."

Tina frowned even as Tyler practically danced on air. He had gone from petulant to delighted in the ninety minutes or so that he'd spent in children's church. "Yeah, Mom. Donovan said he don't got school tomorrow."

"Teacher workday," Ann confirmed. "Dean's going to be over at your place, so we might as well get together at mine."

Wyatt jumped in to explain. "I've contracted Dean to spray the pastures for the worms that cost Dodd his last herd. It's got to be done before the horses and cattle can be purchased."

Tina nodded. "It's just that I have so much work to do at the house."

Wyatt knew Tina well enough by now to recognize the concern that she wore like sackcloth. She worried that Tyler wouldn't behave properly, but Wyatt felt he would be happier with a new friend, especially one like Donovan Pryor.

Wyatt sidled up to Tina, softly encouraging her to agree. "Ty needs a friend his own age." Donovan was a year older, but he was closer in age to Tyler than Frankie.

"I'm sure Frankie would enjoy a morning of play," Jake put in heartily, "provided you're sure he won't be any trouble to include."

Dean hoisted up a flame-haired little girl into his arms, her ruffled skirts fluffing. "Maybe Frankie can entertain Glory," he said hopefully. "Otherwise, Donovan will be toting her everywhere."

"He's a very protective big brother," Ann said with a chuckle. "We had to conspire to keep him away from Glory to get her walking. It will do him good to have some time with a new friend."

"Every anchor to War Bonnet and Loco Man Ranch is a good thing for Tyler," Wyatt whispered.

"What about your lunch?" Tina hedged. "Who'll cook for you guys?"

"We can fend for ourselves once in a while."

"And if you're interested in gardening, Grandma Billie will be only too willing to show you her vegetable patch," Ann prodded. "That way, if you simply must work, you can pull weeds."

Tina laughed, but Wyatt caught the note of tension

in the sound. He placed an encouraging hand on her shoulder. Finally, she gave in.

"How can I turn down such a gracious invitation? Thank you."

Ann smiled brightly. "We'll expect y'all around nine tomorrow morning. All right?"

"Sounds fine," Wyatt confirmed before Tina could change her mind.

The adults said their farewells, and Wyatt slid his hand to the small of Tina's back, urging her toward the church's exit. In truth, Wyatt didn't know if Ty could put aside his resentment and confusion long enough to mind his manners and enjoy the playdate, but he believed wholeheartedly that Ty needed this friendship, and Wyatt expected that the Pryors were more than capable of handling one unhappy little boy if the need arose. Moreover, he felt that Tina could benefit from the relationship, too. He didn't know Ann Pryor very well, but his dealings with the Billings family had shown him that they were solid, caring, generous people. Tina could use a friend like Ann.

What Tina apparently didn't need was him. He walked her to her car and helped Ty into his safety seat. She got into the car and drove away without a single word for him. She'd looked so pretty in her flowered Easter dress. Sighing, he turned toward his truck, only to find his brothers looking at him with lopsided grins on their faces.

"What?" he demanded. "Donovan will be a good influence on Ty."

"You would know," Ryder said. "You and Donovan have that protective big brother thing in common."

Wyatt made a face. So he *liked* being the big brother. Nothing wrong with that.

"Make fun if you want to, but we all know that Tyler needs a friend his own age."

"Uh-huh," Jake said. "That isn't all he needs."

Irked, Wyatt shot back, "It's not that she doesn't try to discipline him. She's doing the best she can in difficult circumstances."

Jake just grinned and turned for the truck.

"He means that, from all you say, Tyler needs a real dad," Ryder explained. "And even Frankie can see who the likeliest candidate for that job is."

Recalling the moment when Frankie had offered Unca Wyatt as Tyler's daddy, Wyatt felt heat burn its way up his neck. Wyatt snatched Frankie from his father's side and lifted the boy into his safety seat. He couldn't help thinking that, for all practical purposes, Frankie had three fathers, all of them fully capable of seeing to his needs. It didn't seem fair that Tyler didn't have even one.

Jake clapped a hand on Wyatt's shoulder. "What Ryder's trying to say is that it takes a good big brother to know one."

"Look, it's about time you thought about someone other than the three of us," Ryder told Wyatt. "Maybe it's time to think about what you want and need."

"So, you think I need a prickly woman soured on marriage and a brat?"

"I think you need—"

"And deserve," Jake interjected.

"—a woman who loves you. And a family of your own."

"*You're* my family," Wyatt said, his voice gravelly with emotion. "You two plus Frankie." Besides, Tina had made it perfectly clear that she couldn't—wouldn't—love him or any man.

"Of course we're your family," Ryder said, "but we're big boys now. You don't have to look after us anymore."

"And you've proved with Frankie that you're a great substitute father," Jake added. "Besides, we didn't stop being family when I married Jolene, did we?"

Wyatt shook his head. "No, Jolene just added to the family, and so did Frankie. I'm not sure it would be the same with Tina and Tyler, though."

"But you want to find out," Jake prodded.

Wyatt shook his head again. "I don't know. I'm not sure she even likes me. In fact, I think she likes you and Ryder better."

Jake laughed. "She's not attracted to either of us. We don't threaten her single existence."

"We see how she looks at you," Ryder teased, "and how you look at her. Go for it, man. What have you got to lose?"

His heart, for one thing. And the odds were certainly against him with Tina. Still, the worst that could happen is that he'd get shot down. It wasn't as if she'd take away anything he already had, anything more than the ranch house and the mineral rights, anyway. He found that he didn't so much mind losing those things now. And his ego could take it if she wasn't interested. He'd just have to keep his heart safely locked away until he knew which way this thing would go.

"We want you to be happy," Jake said.

"And to stop worrying about us," Ryder added urgently.

Too moved to speak, Wyatt slapped each of them lightly on the cheek and got into the truck. Maybe it was time he started thinking about his own future. Jake and Frankie were getting on with life after losing Jolene. Ryder was far removed from the anger and pain of what had happened in Houston. Loco Man Ranch would soon be a real operation again.

Tina said she didn't want a man in her life, but she'd tolerated his interference with Tyler and let him convince her to accept Ann Pryor's invitation. That had to mean that she at least trusted him.

Didn't it?

He supposed he could ask God to guide him and see what happened.

What happened didn't give him much hope. Despite his attempts to engage her in friendly conversation, Tina kept her distance, barely looking at him as she went about her business. Still, he couldn't seem to leave her alone. After a Sunday dinner of baked ham and all the fixings, Tina and the kids dyed eggs. Jake and Ryder went out to hide them while Tina took the boys into the den.

Wyatt wandered in to see what they were watching on Dodd's old TV. The ancient antenna outside received only two stations, but Wyatt had arranged for cable and internet, which would be installed in the next day or two. Meanwhile, Tina had set up a DVD player and several videos appropriate for children. The one currently playing was an animated superhero film. While the boys watched the ridiculously small television screen, Tina sat to one side, reading a book. Wyatt stood there for several minutes, waiting to see if Tina would acknowledge him. He knew perfectly well that she realized he was there, but she neither looked up nor spoke.

Finally, he said, "We have a flat-screen TV that we can hang on the wall there."

"That'll be nice," Tina murmured without looking up from her book.

"Might have some furniture you want to use in here, too. We won't need it all in the bunkhouse."

She turned a page. "Better wait and see what you need first."

Deflated, he left the room. So much for her interest in him.

He watched from the sidelines as the boys hunted for Easter eggs. Then, feeling restless, he went out to the barn and fired up one of the ATVs that Jake had gotten running. After driving around the ranch for a couple of hours, he felt better, but he was still puzzled by all those fenced parcels of grass. He decided to search Dodd's office for any related papers, but the search proved fruitless.

He did, however, find a safety deposit box key. Leaving the key where he found it, Wyatt decided to go down to the bank in town sometime soon to see if the key fit a box there.

When he walked into the kitchen a few minutes later, he found Tina building thick ham sandwiches. He went to the cabinet to get out plates.

"I thought we'd use paper plates tonight," she said without stopping what she was doing. "Less cleanup."

He closed the cabinet door. "Okay. Want to unlock your car, then? I'll transfer Frankie's safety seat from my truck to your car before it gets dark. That way it'll be in place when you're ready to leave for the Pryors' farm tomorrow."

She sent him a look from the corner of her eye as she walked to the small, decorative table next to the back door. Taking her keys from her handbag, she pointed them outside and remotely unlocked her car doors. Then she returned to the sandwiches.

Wyatt removed Frankie's seat from his truck and carried it around to the passenger-side door of the back seat of Tina's little sedan. She came out then to open the vehicle door for him and clear away several items of Tyler's. Wyatt installed the seat, while Tina stood there with her arms folded. He didn't know what was eating her, but he wanted to.

"Dean and Ann Pryor are excellent people," he told her, just for something to say. "All the Billings family are."

"I know that."

"I met Donovan the day I went to talk to Dean about the spraying," Wyatt went on. "I was impressed by the boy's behavior."

"Meaning you think Tyler will benefit from Donovan's example."

Wyatt faced her. "I do think Donovan will be a good influence."

Tina huffed out a sigh. "I never know anymore whether to be offended by your high-handedness or grateful for your concern."

He flattened his lips, choosing his words carefully.

"You can think I'm high-handed if you want, but I meant what I said to Tyler this morning. I won't put up with his disrespect for you or any other adult around here. I can't. Frankie looks up to Tyler."

She lifted her chin, holding his gaze. Then, without another word, she flounced off, heading back into the house.

Wyatt shook his head, but something told him that she wasn't as upset as she wanted either of them to believe. He hit the lock and closed the car door, wondering if he ought to ask Rex about interstate custody petitions. Maybe it would be high-handed of him, but he couldn't see how it would hurt to know the facts, especially when all he wanted to do was help.

Setting aside her tea glass, Tina laughed heartily. She hadn't laughed so much in…she couldn't remember when. Ann's tales of Donovan and his dog, Digger, had kept everyone in stitches for a good hour.

Ann's sister, Meri Burns, had been there when Tina had arrived. They had discussed the upcoming wedding of Ann and Meri's father, and Tina had found herself volunteering to contribute to the effort. Afterward, the women had toured Billie's vegetable patch, which was less a patch and more like a small farm, since it covered at least an acre. Tina had learned plenty to help her with the much smaller garden that she planned to plant on Loco Man Ranch next year. Then Meri had left to put her little one down for a nap and make her husband's lunch. Dean's grandmother, Billie, who lived with Ann and Dean, was considerably younger than Tina had expected. She'd prepared an excellent lunch and offered to teach Tina how to can and freeze her eventual harvest.

Billie and Ann were obviously close. Tina envied them, and she had to admit that Donovan was a good influence on Tyler. Donovan's manners were impeccable, and Tyler eagerly followed his example in an apparent effort to ingratiate himself with the older boy.

The two boys had been playing outside for some time, while Frankie and Glory entertained themselves in the living room. Donovan ran in just then, followed by Tyler, and came to his mother's side, standing quietly until she smiled at him in acknowledgment.

"Can Tyler and me play in my room?"

"Why don't you bring some toys down to the living room, so the younger kids don't feel left out?"

Donovan agreed easily. "Okay. Come on, Ty."

To Tina's surprise and delight, Tyler looked to her and asked, "Is it okay if I help Donovan get his toys?"

"Why, of course you can," Tina replied. "Just be sure that you help pick up the toys after you're through playing with them."

"I promise!" Tyler vowed, rushing off after his friend.

Soon, he and Donovan were racing toy cars around a track while Frankie and little Glory played with a busy center. Frankie pushed the same buttons over and over, and Glory giggled every time. Digger lay at Donovan's side patiently watching the play. From her seat at the dining table, Tina could see that Tyler occasionally reached over and stroked the dog.

She wondered if Wyatt would object if she got a dog for Tyler, then she scolded herself. The house belonged to her. She could get a dog if she wanted one. Thinking of Wyatt made her check the time.

She gasped. "I had no idea it was getting so late."

"Oh, do you have to go so soon?" Ann protested. "We've had such a good time."

"I need to get supper in the oven," Tina said regretfully.

"That reminds me. I need to pull a casserole out of the freezer," Billie Pryor proclaimed. "Where is my head today?" She rose from her chair.

"Where it always is," Ann countered affectionately. "Wrapped around taking care of this family."

"You have the kids to look after and the business," Billie said, heading for the kitchen.

"The business?" Tina queried, smiling at Ann.

"Our custom farming business," Ann answered. "I just handle the books and scheduling. Dean does nearly all the tilling, planting and harvesting in this county, along with a lot of other things. Because equipment is absurdly expensive, local farmers are happy to pay Dean to do the work. They don't have to borrow money for equipment, and we're showing profit. We've also put in our own crops for the past two years now, which means my husband works much too hard."

"Honey, that man wouldn't know any other way to work," Billie said as she returned. "Besides, it takes a hardworking man to make it out here."

"True," Ann agreed. "Dean wouldn't be happy with any other life, though, and I wouldn't be happy if he wasn't happy. Meri does pretty much the same thing for Stark that I do for Dean."

"That's the way it is out here," Billie said. "Takes

everyone pitching in to make this life work. It's a good life, though."

Nodding, Ann smiled. Tina couldn't help thinking of Wyatt and his brothers. While Layne had complained about having to return phone calls, preferred to sleep late and painted only when conditions were exactly right, the Smith brothers got up early every morning and went to work happily with no complaints. None of them ever seemed to lack for work, either. While she kept Ryder busy in the house, Jake had completely reconfigured the bunkhouse, and Wyatt had gone from research to repairing the barn and corrals and purchasing tack and equipment. Just today he'd gone out to buy a cattle hauler, after discovering that Dodd's old trailer had rusted clear through. Now that they had cable and internet service—the technician had arrived as Tina and the children were leaving this morning—Wyatt would be setting up books and accounts on his computer next.

Thinking of all that Wyatt and his brothers were doing, Tina got to her feet. "I really have to go, but I've so enjoyed myself."

"We're very glad you came."

"So am I." She got to her feet and went into the living room, Ann following, just in time to hear Donovan say, "That stinks. My first mom didn't want me, but it's okay. Dad wants me lots, and Ann's my real mom, anyhow."

Momentarily stunned by the topic the two boys were discussing, Tina whipped a glance at Ann, who simply smiled and whispered, "It's true. Dean would've married her, but she just handed over the baby and apparently never looked back." Obviously, the subject wasn't a secret in the Pryor household.

"My mommy in Heaven," Frankie said matter-of-factly. "Maybe she come back."

"That won't happen," Tyler informed Frankie bluntly. "No one comes back from Heaven."

"Nor would we want them to," Tina interrupted, fearing Frankie's reaction. "Heaven is a wonderful place, and everyone there is very happy."

Frankie frowned, then yawned.

"Someone seems ready for a nap," Ann remarked with a chuckle.

Tina crouched before Frankie. "Would you like to go home and take a nap now?"

He nodded, rubbed his eyes and reached for her. She gathered him up, standing with him on her hip. Like all the Smith males, he was large and his weight nearly staggered her, but she remembered happily how it had felt when Tyler had reached for her, begging to be held. Looking down, she saw the envy on Tyler's face and felt a jolt of joy. He remembered those times, too. If only his father would stop trying to poison him against her, they could have a lovely relationship. Still, she knew the days of him wanting to be held were behind them.

She knew she would never have that particular experience again.

Unless she remarried and had more children of her own.

But she was already blessed with one son. She wouldn't ask for more.

Smiling, she set Frankie on his feet and addressed Tyler. "Help Donovan clean up, sweetie, so we can go."

"Aw, Mo-om," Tyler whined, but he started helping Donovan break apart the racetrack and stow the pieces in a plastic tub.

Ann added the busy center to the tub and picked up Glory, saying, "Thank you, Tyler. Donovan will take the toys upstairs."

To Tina's surprise, Donovan got up and hugged both her and Frankie. "Bye, Mizz Kemp."

"Goodbye, Donovan."

Not to be outdone, Tyler leaped up and ran over to give Ann a quick hug. "Bye, Mizz Pryor."

"Goodbye, Tyler, and thank you for coming."

"Thank you for having us," Tina replied.

Tyler looked at Donovan. "Maybe you can come to my house tomorrow."

"Not tomorrow," Ann said, "but soon."

Dissatisfied with that, Tyler began to whine again. "But when? Why not?"

"Donovan has school tomorrow," Tina quickly pointed out, "but we'll set up another playdate soon."

Tyler bowed his head in obvious disgust, but he didn't protest further.

As she drove back to Loco Man Ranch, Tina thought about all that had happened. Wyatt had been right on every count. Ann and her family were wonderful people. Tina was grateful to have made friends with her and her sister, and she was thrilled that Tyler wanted to emulate Donovan's behavior. She'd never met a better behaved, more loving, well-adjusted child than Donovan.

Looking into the rearview mirror, Tina said to her

son, "You made me proud today, Tyler. You behaved very well. And I promise you'll get to see Donovan again as soon as possible."

Smiling slightly, he nodded and turned his head to gaze out the window.

Yes, Wyatt had been right. Again. Tina was coming to realize that he usually was.

She couldn't help wishing that she had met Wyatt first. If it had been him instead of Layne…

She shook her head.

Why wish for the impossible?

It was enough that she and Tyler had Wyatt and his brothers in their lives now.

# Chapter Nine

As soon as Tina brought her car to a stop at the ranch, Frankie sat up straight and looked around. He spied Wyatt walking toward the house from the barn and pointed. "Unca Wyatt! Unca Wyatt, get me."

Chuckling, Tina got out and walked around to let the boy out of his safety harness while Tyler unclipped his own belt and opened his own car door. Waving to Wyatt, she called out to him. "I think Frankie wants you to put him to bed for a nap."

Wyatt lengthened his stride and was standing next to her by the time Frankie crawled down from his seat. Tyler came around to join them.

"Did you guys have fun?" Wyatt asked.

"It was a blast!" Tyler exclaimed.

Frankie just nodded and lifted both arms in a silent plea for Wyatt to hold him. Wyatt easily swung the boy up against his chest.

"Unca Wyatt," Frankie asked solemnly, "my mama come back from Heaven?"

Wyatt curled a finger under the boy's chin. "Who told you your mama would come back from Heaven?"

Cringing inwardly, Tina shook her head. "I'm afraid Tyler told him that his mother would *not* come back from Heaven."

"I didn't mean to," Tyler whined plaintively.

Tina sent him a look before turning her attention back to Wyatt. "I don't know how they got on the subject. Donovan said that his first mother didn't want him but that it was okay, because his dad does want him and Ann is his real mother. That's when Frankie said his mother might come back from Heaven, and Tyler told him that wouldn't happen."

Apparently unruffled, Wyatt looked to Tyler. "Well, these things happen. Kids talk. We expect Frankie to have questions from time to time." He smoothed Frankie's curly hair. "Frankie, do you remember your mother?"

Frankie pondered a moment, his finger stealing into his mouth, then he laid his head on Wyatt's shoulder. Wyatt and Tina exchanged glances. Clearly, the boy had no firm images of his mother, but perhaps he remembered the warmth of her arms or the sound of her voice. Apparently, he missed her more than anyone had realized.

Wyatt patted him and said, "Let's go talk to your dad. He usually has a photo of your mom on him."

Wyatt carried Frankie toward the bunkhouse. Tina shoved the car door closed, grabbed Tyler by the hand and hurried to catch up with them.

"Do you mind if we tag along? Tyler caused this, after all, and he needs to make an apology."

Wyatt glanced at Tyler. "I don't think Jake will mind you two being there."

She fell in beside them, taking two steps to every one of Wyatt's, Tyler trailing at the end of her arm. Wyatt slowed down to accommodate her and Tyler, so that they walked side by side. For some reason that small gallantry moved her. She tried to remember if Layne had ever made such adjustments for them, but she mostly just remembered trailing along behind him with Tyler in a stroller. It had seemed perfectly natural at the time. Now it seemed telling.

They reached the bunkhouse. Jake had added a pair of steps and a sizable front deck. Someone had arranged a pair of rusty, old metal lawn chairs to one side of the door. Wyatt pulled open the new screen door and stepped inside.

Jake stood atop a ladder in the small front room, connecting a ceiling vent to a wide, flexible insulated hose. The living area couldn't have been more than ten feet square, much too small for five people and a ladder, let alone for three big men to relax in comfortably. She knew from supper conversation that Jake had made a space for a small two-burner stove and three or four running feet of cabinet and countertop in a nook just around the corner. The brothers had discussed how to fit a sink into the small space. She hadn't given much thought to the size of the old bunkhouse, but she was beginning to realize that with a kitchenette, bathroom and three bedrooms, the place was going to be cramped at best.

"You about got that central air hooked up?" Wyatt asked.

"Yeah, but I won't turn it on until I get the ceiling in," Jake said, still looking up. "No point in cooling the rafters."

"When you're done there," Wyatt said, "Frankie wants to talk to you."

Jake glanced down then back up at the clamp he was tightening. "This should do it." He dropped a small screwdriver into the pocket of his leather tool belt and began backing down the ladder, speaking to his son as he did so. "Did you have fun at the Pryors'?"

Frankie nodded and looked to his uncle, who said, "Let's have a seat on the porch."

He carried the boy back outside and sat down in one of the old lawn chairs with Frankie on his lap. The old metal chair creaked ominously but held their combined weight. Tina took a spot on the corner of the porch. Tyler stood next to Wyatt's chair, patting Frankie on the shoulder.

Heavy gray clouds gathered in the east, but it would be some time before the rain reached them. Meanwhile, the air felt unusually still and thick.

"It seems that Frankie has been thinking his mom might come back from Heaven to visit us one day," Wyatt said as Jake took the chair beside him.

Jake glanced at Wyatt and Tina before pulling Frankie onto his lap. "We'll see your mama again someday, son, but in Heaven, not here on earth."

"She don't come back?" Frankie asked.

"No, son. She won't come back, but we'll all go there, not all at the same time, but one by one until we're all together again. I don't think she'd want us to come too soon, though, because when we go there, we won't come back here until we all come with Jesus."

"With Jesus," Frankie parroted.

"That's right," Wyatt said. "Mommy's with Jesus, and we'll all be with Him someday, too."

"I wan' see her," Frankie said, holding out his hand.

"I think he'd like to see a picture of her," Wyatt explained.

Jake took out his wallet and pulled a photo from behind a plastic window. He passed the small photo to Frankie. "That's you and your mama the day we brought you home from the hospital."

Frankie studied the photo and touched it with a damp finger. "She smilin'."

"She was very happy that day," Jake told him. "She's happy now, too. She loves you very much, but she's happy with Jesus in Heaven."

"Okay," Frankie said, hooking an arm around his father's neck and laying his head on Jake's chest, the photo still clutched in his grubby little hand.

Jake hugged the boy. "We'll put a framed picture of her in our room," he said to Frankie, "so we can see her every morning and every night. What do you think of that?"

"Okay," Frankie said again. He yawned widely.

"Looks like you need a nap, little man," Jake said. "Want to take a nap in here with me? I've got a sleeping bag you can use."

Frankie nodded, yawning again.

Jake tapped him on the end of his nose. "I think you were so excited about going over to Donovan's today that you didn't sleep much last night."

Frankie just closed his eyes and sighed. Tyler went over and patted Frankie's shoulder again. Jake looked at Wyatt and Tina.

"I hope he behaved himself today," he said to Tina, and she nodded.

"Oh, yes." She smiled at Tyler, pleased that he seemed to realize he'd blundered and wanted to comfort Frankie as best he could. "They both did." Tyler stood a little straighter.

"You put him down for a nap. We'll talk later," Wyatt told Jake softly. Nodding, Jake got to his feet and carried his son into the bunkhouse to the room they would soon share on a permanent basis.

Tina felt a pang of guilt at the idea. It wasn't right. Tyler had his own room; Frankie ought to have one of his own, not to mention Jake. She bit her lip, pondering the situation. All along, the Smith brothers had been helpful and cooperative. No doubt, from their point of view, they'd gotten a raw deal when Dodd had left the house to her, but they'd adapted and been pleasant about it.

They were the kind of men she wanted her son to emulate: hardworking, caring, responsible and churchgoing. Layne's idea of attending church was putting in an appearance at Easter or Christmas. If he couldn't manage to get out of it.

But how did she broach what she was thinking now? How did she ask three unmarried men to live with her and her son?

Especially when she couldn't seem to stop thinking about one of them in particular?

Tina slid off the porch and stood up. Tyler jumped

down next to her. Wyatt walked down the two steps and took her by the elbow, pointing her toward the house. Tyler rushed to walk on his other side, and Wyatt laid a hand on his back.

"We're sorry this happened," Tina said.

Wyatt looked down at Tyler. "There was no malicious intent, and I doubt this is the last time Frankie will have questions about his mom."

"You and Jake are both so good with Frankie," Tina said. "Ryder, too. I noticed that from the very beginning."

"We all love that boy. Ryder and I cared for him when Jake and Jolene were both deployed."

"I didn't know they could do that," Tina said. "Deploy both parents at the same time."

"It was a four month mission for Jolene, and she got a promotion out of it. Then she died stateside in a training accident a few weeks after her return. I thank God we were there for Jake and Frankie during that awful time."

"So do I," she told him, "but it's more than just being family. You genuinely like having Frankie around."

"Why wouldn't we?"

"Lots of men don't like having kids around."

Wyatt chuckled. "That's just laziness. Or selfishness. Maybe both."

"Yes, I see that. I just wish more fathers were like the three of you." She sighed. "Children follow the examples set for them." Sometimes Tyler came home from Layne's saying the most awful things. He'd been sent home from school once for repeating something Layne had said in front of him.

"If parents don't teach kids acceptable behavior," Wyatt said, "life will. Someone somewhere will take exception to unacceptable words and actions."

"I'm just glad that the Smith brothers set a good example."

"We try to. Thank you for noticing."

She turned to look at him. "How could I not?" Glancing at the bunkhouse, she made a decision. "I was thinking, Wyatt, that it might be best if you all stayed in the house with us. The bunkhouse is too small for the four of you."

He stepped back, seeming genuinely shocked. "What are you suggesting, Tina? That we stop work on the bunkhouse now?"

Shaking her head, she said, "We could always rent out the bunkhouse, as a sort of annex to the main house."

"There's only seven bedrooms in the house and you're splitting some of them into bathrooms."

"I know, but we could fix up the attic, too. That would give us two bedrooms in the house to rent plus the bunkhouse."

He stroked his chin. "I don't know. The bathroom in the bunkhouse is super tiny. Jake took the space out of it for the kitchen."

"We could split the corner bedroom into two private baths, one for each of the remaining bedrooms, and use the current bathroom to enlarge the kitchen. The footprint would have to be changed a bit, but it could be done. Couldn't it?"

"That way everyone gets his or her own bedroom,

and you'll have four rooms to rent—two in the house, two in the bunkhouse."

"I think it's the best solution all around."

"Maybe Ryder and I should take the bunkhouse, let Frankie and Jake take rooms in the main house."

"Or maybe Jake and Frankie would like to have their own place in the bunkhouse," Tina suggested casually. "We can work this out any number of ways."

Smiling down at her, Wyatt nodded his approval. "I'll talk it over with Jake and Ryder, and let you know."

Tina turned toward the house again and felt Wyatt's hand settle in the small of her back. Together, they casually strolled toward the door.

Feeling that she'd done the right thing, Tina had never enjoyed a simple walk more.

Tyler's presence made it difficult for Wyatt to tell Tina what he'd learned from Rex that day about interstate custody fights. He noticed that when Tina suggested Tyler fetch his crayons and a coloring book and keep her company while she started supper, the boy readily agreed. He noticed, too, how pleased Tina was by Tyler's instant agreement. Things seemed to be improving there. Taking advantage of the moment, Wyatt stepped close to Tina.

"Can we talk later? After Tyler goes to bed?"

She blinked at that, but nodded. "Sure. What about?"

"I'd rather not get into it now." He didn't want to include Tyler in what should be an adult conversation, and if she was going to fuss and fume about Wyatt's high-handedness, he'd rather she did it in private. "Besides, I need to get on the computer."

"Okay."

"By the way, I've arranged for the moving truck to arrive in a couple weeks. We've cleaned out a suitable space in the barn to store what we can't use right now."

"All right."

He smiled and said, "You know, we've got two refrigerators, and neither of them are going to fit in the bunkhouse."

Looking at the ancient little fridge at the end of the cabinet, she retorted dryly, "I guess we'll just have to find a place for them." They both laughed.

Tyler returned then, a heap of coloring books under one arm and a shoebox-sized tin of crayons in the other. Wyatt took himself off to Dodd's office and got busy. Listening idly to Tina and Tyler in the kitchen, Wyatt set up his laptop. He'd previously cleared away the stacks of papers littering the old desk, using a pair of boxes as filing drawers.

Dodd hadn't been much for filing. He'd left a box labeled Tax that contained receipts and such, and another filled with unopened bank statements, which Wyatt had been gradually working through. Nothing in either box told Wyatt anything about Dodd's intention with the fenced acres of sowed grass, but they did tell another story.

Dodd's financial situation had been alarmingly precarious. He'd had less than a thousand dollars in the ranch account. He'd used his Social Security to pay the utilities and buy groceries. He could've hung on for another year, at least, and then he could have sold acreage to pay taxes. No one would have blamed him. Wyatt could only imagine that Dodd had been experimenting with varieties of grass that wouldn't host worms, in the hope of somehow being able to restock. Maybe the veterinarian, Stark Burns, knew something about that. Wyatt had made an appointment for Stark to inspect the range after Dean finished the spraying. He would ask Stark what he knew then.

Meanwhile, Rex had told Wyatt where to download software to help track everything from expenses to well-animal treatments and veterinary visits. Rex had talked a lot about ranch-fed beef, too. He made a good case for raising one's own fodder rather than buying manufactured feeds or using feed lots. For Loco Man, those were decisions for the coming year, not this one.

Tina showed up in the open doorway to say that supper was ready. He lost no time in closing out the program he'd set up and heading for the kitchen, where he found Tyler setting plates on the table. Frankie followed him, placing forks next to each plate. Jake reached over them to set glasses of tea on the table.

"You've got a couple of good helpers here," Wyatt told Tina, winking at the boys. Ty beamed at him. "I'm not sure about the tall one, though."

"He stinks," Frankie stated matter-of-factly, and everyone but Jake laughed.

"All right, all right. I'll go clean up," Jake grumbled, scowling despite the mirth glinting in his eyes.

"Wait," Tina said, waving Jake and everyone else to the table. "All of you. You're fine, and I won't be happy if you let this meal get cold."

Jake eagerly pulled out a chair. Ryder came in and went to wash up in the bathroom. Wyatt pulled out a chair for Tina, then went to wash up at the kitchen sink. Tina sat so Jake would. He lifted Frankie onto his boosted seat and pulled the chair close to the table.

They enjoyed a fine meal. Afterward, Wyatt and Ryder helped Tina clean up the dishes while Jake got the boys ready for bed. Then the boys played in Tyler's room with Ryder and Jake tried out the new cable TV. Wyatt caught Tina's eye and nodded toward the front of the house. The two of them slipped out onto the porch.

"What did you want to talk about?" she asked as soon as he pulled the door closed behind them.

Wyatt took a deep breath. "Now, don't bite my head off, but I spoke to Rex about what's involved in a custody battle like yours."

To his relief, Tina merely nodded. "And?"

"And it could be a very expensive proposition for both parties."

Tina wandered across the porch to sit on the steps. The days were getting longer, and it wasn't dark enough for more than a bit of moon and a few stars to show through the gloaming. Wyatt walked over and sat down next to her.

"I know that's not what you want to hear."

She shook her head, studying her fingernails. "I told you before. Layne is heir to a large family fortune. He can do as he pleases."

"And you've got just what you're investing in this place," Wyatt surmised gently.

"That's about it."

He balanced his forearms against his thighs, hands linked. "I'm sorry, Tina."

"Not your fault."

"I'll help any way I can."

A wan smile quirked her pretty lips, but she didn't look at him. "Thanks, but I don't know what you could do."

"I can pray, at least."

In a strained voice, she said, "I hope your prayers have more power than mine." Suddenly, she wiped tears from her eyes. "I can't tell you how many times I've prayed for God's intervention, only to be disappointed."

Reaching for her hand, he stayed silent, letting her talk.

"Every time my mother married, I prayed it would be the last time. That my new stepfather would want me as a daughter as much as he wanted her as a wife, but that never happened with anyone but Dodd, and she left him. She just couldn't stay interested in any one man. She had five husbands. Five."

"You don't need serial marriages to make you happy," Wyatt said softly. "Just one. The right one."

"Maybe. But I obviously got her judgment genes. Look who I picked."

"You must've been young when you married him."

"Twenty-one. Just barely."

"It's easy to be swept off your feet that young."

"I was in my junior year of college, but I really hadn't dated much." She shrugged. "I didn't want to make a mistake, but when this handsome, successful artist who'd lectured in one of my classes asked me out, I thought he was the answer to my prayers. A few months later, my mother died. I—I had no one and nowhere to go. I hadn't seen my father since I was ten.

When Layne asked me to marry him, I—I thought God was telling me he was the one."

"Why are you so certain He wasn't?" Wyatt asked. "What's best for us isn't something we can easily decide for ourselves. We have to trust that God knows best."

"You think Layne was best for me?" she asked incredulously.

"Maybe at the time. Without him, you wouldn't have had Tyler."

"That's true," she admitted.

"Without a doubt, you had to be what was best for Layne," Wyatt said evenly.

She cocked her head, looking at him with intense interest. "What do you mean by that?"

"You were Layne's chance to be the man he should be. It's not your fault he didn't take advantage of the opportunity. It's your fault if you don't take advantage of the opportunities God gives you."

Wyatt could tell by the look on her face that she had never considered such a possibility.

Gradually, her features softened, her big, coppery eyes filling with sadness for what might have been.

She squeezed Wyatt's hand, warming his heart with that simple gesture.

"Thank you."

He knew then that he wanted more from Tina than simple friendship or a business partnership. He didn't know why he hadn't seen it from the beginning, but that didn't matter now. She did.

Without a clue as to how it had happened, he knew that she mattered now.

Very much.

## Chapter Ten

For a long moment, Wyatt couldn't seem to break eye contact with Tina. He had completely misjudged her in the beginning. She wasn't selfish and entitled. Her prickliness was a result of her hesitancy to trust, and who could blame her, given what she'd been through? They had both lost their mothers at a young age, but he'd had fifteen years of calm, loving, wise support to prepare him for the loss. Tina had had only disappointment and instability. Yet, as a mother herself, she was a calm, loving, wise support for her son and doing her best to give him the stability that she had lacked.

It saddened Wyatt to realize that everyone she'd ever trusted had betrayed her in some way, even Dodd to a degree. What had that old man been thinking to leave her his house while seeing to it that his nephews owned the very ground it sat on? Given her situation, she must have been horrified. Yet, she had cooperated in every possible way, even if unhappily at first. She had to be as puzzled by Dodd's actions as Wyatt and his brothers.

Dodd had always had a funny way of reasoning, but

he usually had figured out what was needed. Wyatt couldn't for the life of him understand what the old man had been trying to accomplish with this will situation. Had he simply wanted to remember Tina in some way? Had he expected Wyatt and his brothers to buy her out? Or was something else going on here?

An odd thought struck him. Had Dodd been matchmaking? He'd rambled on and on about Walker, but Wyatt hadn't paid much attention. In his mind, Walker had been a mere acquaintance of Dodd's, not someone Dodd had loved. Eventually, she'd become just another name associated with the ranch, like Delgado. Wyatt hadn't given her much more thought than that. Now he wondered if Dodd had hoped that one of his nephews would realize what a special lady this beautiful woman truly was.

She suddenly laughed gently, rolling her eyes.

"What? What's so funny?"

"I was just thinking of Frankie offering you to Tyler as a substitute father. Out of the mouths of babes, right?" She shook her head. "If only it were that easy. If only I could say, 'We'll take this one instead.' It would be so simple if there was a father store. 'This one comes with good sense, authority and genuine concern. This one is a good provider, a hard worker, kind.' Wonder if I could get a money-back guarantee?"

"Maybe you could upgrade every time a new version came out, like cell phones," Wyatt teased, but she shook her head, her eyes suddenly wide.

"Uh, no. That was my mother's approach."

Wyatt spread his hands, trying to get the conversation back on track and away from the source of her fears. "I was actually pleased that Frankie came up with that. He was pretty attached to me when Jake came home. I think it hurt Jake a lot. Maybe it was just losing Jolene, but there were times when Frankie reached for me instead of his father, and Jake's pain was tangible. I felt like I was walking a tightrope, trying to comfort and care for Frankie and subtly shift his dependence to Jake at the same time."

"While you love them both."

"Of course. That's the bottom line, isn't it? There are no perfect dad stores, no perfect uncles, either. There's just love to cover all the inadequacies."

"I loved Layne," she whispered. "It wasn't enough."

"It takes two to keep that kind of love alive, two people willing to work and forgive and make each other a priority. My folks used to say that they were a single unit and they had to work to keep their connection healthy and whole. Then together they put God first and their children second. As individuals, they put themselves at the bottom of the list. It's an imperfect analogy, but they made it work. Their relationship was so solid that my dad was never the same after he lost her, but he wouldn't have had it any other way. He loved her without end, and I know she loved him the same way."

"That's beautiful," Tina said, her eyes shining.

"*You're* beautiful," Wyatt heard himself say to her.

She blinked those big, glittering eyes at him. He wanted to kiss her. Obeying the impulse, he lifted his hand to the back of her head. He felt the sleek, clean strands of her short hair and the warmth of her skin beneath as he captured her mouth with his.

She stiffened for an instant, and then she melted into his arms.

*Mine*, he thought. *This is what it's all about.*

Excitement flooded his veins, bolstered by a soaring hope. That kiss became something precious and momentous. His future seemed to be taking shape before his mind's eye. Then suddenly Tina shoved against him, and before he knew what was happening, she stood halfway across the porch.

"No!" she exclaimed, trembling. "No. I—I won't go from man to man. I'm not…"

Not her mother. She didn't have to say it.

Wyatt rose to his feet, twisting around to face her. He kept his movements slow and easy, his tone gentle and even. "Tina. Sweetheart. You're not—" the next instant, he was talking to air "—anything like her." The door closed between them before the words were hardly out of his mouth.

He ran his hands over his face. Well, he couldn't have blown that any worse with dynamite.

"You want to come out to the bunkhouse and see what we've done with the furniture you sent there?"

Wyatt stood just outside Ryder's bedroom door in the upstairs hallway, his expression guarded. Shaking her head, Tina turned her attention back to the bed she was making up. The Smith goods had arrived and been dispersed as she had designated. The old fridge had gone to the bunkhouse. Two new stainless steel versions replaced it: one in the kitchen, the other in the laundry room. With electricity and new appliances, they were starting to live in the twenty-first century once again.

While something of a mishmash, all the furniture was of good quality and comfortable, and just having the things in the house made the whole place feel more like home. She had reluctantly let go of the rickety antiques and filled the parlor with comfy, overstuffed leather couches. The boys were thrilled with the huge flat-screen television now hanging on the wall, especially with the cable working. Plus, they had real beds and fresh linens for all the bedrooms, not to mention dressers for storage and even a lovely cheval glass that had belonged to Frances Smith. Tina had set aside Dodd's old kitchen table to use as a desk and replaced it with Wyatt's long, rectangular wrought-iron one. She loved its terracotta tile top, which had fired her imagination for remodeling the kitchen. Jake's warm oak dining set, with its spacious buffet, now occupied the dining room, though the inexpensive drapes she'd hung in there no longer felt appropriate.

In so many ways, the old house had come to life. Tyler certainly seemed better satisfied. Still, she had more important things to do just now than worry about furniture placement.

"I'll worry about that later. Just be sure you don't damage anything with the painting and finish work. When I'm done here, I need to start calling contractors. Ryder can't go much further until the roof is repaired, and we have rain in the forecast again. I need to bring in a professional ASAP. There's the plumbing and bathroom fixtures to be installed, too." She stopped smoothing and tucking the sheets and straightened, lifting the back of her hand to her forehead, her mind whirling. "I won't know how much money I'll have for decorating until the essential work is done, so there's no point in worrying about the bunkhouse now."

Behind her, she heard Wyatt's feet shift on the hardwood floor. That reminded her she needed the floors refinished, too. So much to do. Yet, she knew she was mainly looking for ways to avoid Wyatt.

All they'd done for nearly two weeks now was avoid each other. Ever since that kiss on the front porch. The one she couldn't seem to forget. Giving the sheet one more tug, she placed her other hand on her hip. Avoidance was surprisingly hard work, especially when she wasn't sleeping well.

Lately, no matter how hard she worked during the daytime, she tossed and turned at night. Maybe if she didn't dream during her brief moments of sleep, she'd have more energy. That kiss wouldn't leave her mind, though. She remembered all too well the rise of joy in her heart, the warmth of his embrace.

She dreamed of that kiss. She dreamed of his strong arms cradling her against him as if she was the most precious thing in his world. Then suddenly Wyatt would turn into Layne; Layne's arms holding her, Layne's expensive cologne overwhelming her. In her dreams, she could not get away. She struggled frantically, only to wake twisted in the bed covers, her chest heaving in panic. Alone was better than trapped with a selfish, abusive, hateful man.

Deep down, she knew that Wyatt was nothing like Layne, but she couldn't seem to convince herself that he wouldn't eventually act just as hatefully as Layne.

Shaking her head, she pushed away memories of her ex, the dream and the kiss.

With one last glance around the room, she headed for the door, relieved that Wyatt had disappeared. She hurried along the hallway to the stairs. In her haste, she almost tripped on the steps. Remembering how her mother had fallen, she slowed down. Moving over to the table that she'd claimed for her desk, she opened her laptop to get online.

Moments later, she perused a list of available contractors in the area, jotting down phone numbers and making notes. Lyons and Son was the only local option. They'd already been recommended to her, but she made a few other calls first.

A couple of the contractors couldn't give her an estimate for more than a month. Others did not handle roofing or plumbing or floor refinishing but offered to give her numbers for subcontractors they used, some from as far away as Oklahoma City and Wichita Falls, Texas. One fellow drove down from Duncan that afternoon. Lyons admitted they were busy, but because she was local, they promised someone would stop by in the early evening.

Both men listened attentively to her needs and plans. They promised detailed estimates the next day. Both had impeccable references, and their approaches were similar. Tina felt inclined to go with Dixon Lyons, the son in Lyons and Son, simply because he was local, but she couldn't afford to make a mistake, and she knew that if she asked any of the lifelong locals, they'd recommend Lyons. As newcomers, Wyatt and his brothers might be more unbiased, but she didn't want to ask

Wyatt. She had enough trouble just sitting at the dinner table with him. On the other hand, excluding him from any conversation on the subject would be even more awkward than ignoring him.

Ann had encouraged her to attend prayer meetings on Wednesday nights, and suddenly that felt like a good idea tonight. God didn't seem to pay much attention to her one-on-one, but maybe He'd hear her better in church. Maybe He'd pay more attention if hers wasn't the only voice calling out to him. Maybe, in this instance, God would give her obvious direction and guidance.

The Smith brothers routinely attended prayer meetings, but Tina had thus far resisted the midweek service. She'd started to wonder if she wasn't being somewhat petty. Was she staying away because God hadn't answered her prayers the way she wanted? What did that say about her faith?

*What's best for us isn't something we can easily decide for ourselves. We have to trust that God knows best.*

She wanted to believe that she trusted God to do what was best for her, but Wyatt's comments had made her wonder if she wasn't substituting her judgment for God's. Previously, she'd told herself that she hadn't attended prayer meeting because she didn't want to spend more time than necessary in Wyatt's company. But wasn't that just another way of saying God had put her in the wrong position? Or had she put herself there by ignoring God's will?

She needed reassurance that God was listening and had a purpose for all that was happening in her life.

Staying home and keeping so busy that she had no time to think would not provide such reassurance. Something had to give. Still, she dithered on making the decision until after supper that evening.

As usual, Wyatt and his brothers had knocked off work early enough to change before the meal. Jake even got Frankie cleaned up and dressed. Usually the boys put on their pajamas after their baths, but after that first Wednesday here, Jake had made a point of taking Frankie with him to church. It was only an hour, as he pointed out, so it didn't delay the boy's bedtime. Tina had refused Jake's offer to bathe Tyler along with Frankie. If she decided to go to prayer meeting, she could bathe Tyler afterward. Meanwhile, she wouldn't have to decide just yet whether to put Tyler into his pajamas or street clothes.

She mulled the decision all during the meal preparations, gradually becoming aware of a deep need for spiritual solace, and she knew that she was fighting the urge to attend the service simply because Wyatt would be involved. She couldn't face staying home while the others went to church, however. Not again. She had to go. She just had to attend prayer meeting tonight.

The instant the decision was made, she felt overwhelming relief. She placed a bowl of corn on the table and announced, "I think Tyler and I will attend prayer meeting tonight. Ann's been inviting me, and I know Tyler would like to see Donovan again."

Jake, Ryder and Tyler all made approving statements, but Wyatt said nothing. When she dared to glance over at him, however, she found him staring at her with a gentle smile on his face and warmth in his eyes. Delight mixed with panic welled up in her, and she quickly averted her gaze. But she wouldn't change her mind. He reached for the corn, and she pulled out a heavy wrought-iron chair to take her place at the long table.

The meal progressed in near silence, with everyone concentrating on cleaning their plates and getting out of the house on time. Afterward, everyone pitched in to make the cleanup go rapidly. Then Tina grabbed up her handbag and led the way out the back door. She knew she'd dressed better than usual today because she'd intended to go to church all along. Wondering how often she lied to herself, she reached back to encourage Tyler to hurry. That was when her son threw a monkey wrench into the works again.

"I wanna ride with the guys!"

Tina looked down at him with exasperation. His behavior had improved significantly of late, but he still demanded his way from time to time. Usually, she could negotiate a compromise without too much trouble, but time was short just then. She prepared to lay down the law and suffer the consequences, but before she could speak, Wyatt did.

"I can move his seat to my truck. Jake can drive, and I'll ride with you. If that's okay."

Tina desperately wanted to refuse, but Tyler deserved some reward for his recent behavior. And if she were truthful, she longed for the ease she'd had with Wyatt before that kiss. They didn't have to talk about personal matters.

Tyler waited hopefully for her decision.

"Up to you," Wyatt murmured.

She told herself that she and Wyatt could discuss the contractors. Abruptly, she realized that she trusted Wyatt's opinion and advice above all others. And why shouldn't she, after witnessing the way he was going about getting Loco Man Ranch back into production?

She addressed her son. "All right. Wyatt will bring your car seat."

Pressing the tiny remote control in her hand, she unlocked the car and moved to the driver's door while Wyatt slipped around her to access Tyler's safety seat. He had plenty of experience installing such seats because of Frankie, so he made quick work of the change and soon returned to sit down in the front passenger seat.

She didn't give him a chance to say anything before she brought up the subject she'd convinced herself should be the focus of their conversation. "I can't make up my mind which contractor to use."

"Oh?"

She started the car and began backing around to follow Jake in Wyatt's truck. "They both seem entirely capable, and I haven't seen the estimates yet, but one of them is local and the other is out of Duncan."

Wyatt considered the matter as she drove. "The estimates will tell you a lot. If one is much lower than the other, you have to wonder if someone's bumping up his price or if the other is intentionally underestimating."

"Either could be disastrous."

"Exactly. If they're close, you have to consider which one you feel you can best work with."

She shot him an inquisitive glance. "And how am I

to do that? I don't know either of them well enough to make that sort of judgment."

"You may know more about them than you realize. For instance, did either show bias in any way? Some contractors can be dismissive or even disdainful of women."

She shook her head, keeping her gaze trained out the front windshield. "Both were completely respectful."

"Glad to hear it. Well, then, did either question your instructions or plans?"

She thought over her conversations with both men. "No, not really. Each one made suggestions and comments. They each pointed out the same concerns, so obviously I should take those seriously."

"Sounds wise. Did either act as if you might not be able to understand their reasoning? Was either reluctant to explain his conclusions?"

"Actually, one of them was all too willing to explain every little detail, but when I told him that details could be left for later, he just smiled, nodded and shut up."

Wyatt chuckled. "Smart fellow. He understands that you're the boss."

"Oh. I guess so."

"Sounds like either one would do nicely," Wyatt said. "All things being equal, I'd go with the local guy. It never hurts to create goodwill in the town where you live."

"I thought that, too. I just don't want to discount the other man because he doesn't live in War Bonnet."

Wyatt gave her a curious look, one she couldn't quite discern. "I applaud your fairness. But something has to tip the balance."

"True."

"Is the local contractor by any chance Lyons and Son?"

"Yes. Why do you ask?"

"I've heard only good things about them."

"Me, too."

"I haven't met Lyons or his son, but Dixon, I think his name is, was pointed out to me in the diner not too long ago, him and his wife. They had a baby with them, too little to walk yet, but Delgado said she was his sister. Apparently, they're raising her as their own."

"That speaks well for them," Tina remarked.

"I thought so. Unless Lyons does something unexpected with the estimate, I'd say that's the way to go."

She smiled. "I agree. Thanks for your input."

"My pleasure."

They drove in silence for a minute or two before Wyatt said, "Actually, I want to talk to you about something."

*Oh, man, here it comes*, she thought grimly. *He's going to bring up the kiss.*

Hoping to stop him, she spoke. "Can this wait until—"

At the same time, he said, "I've discussed it with my brothers, and—"

Mortified, Tina squawked, "What? You discussed it with your brothers?"

He stared at her, clearly puzzled, until she turned her gaze back out the windshield.

"We're willing to help pay for the renovation."

Shocked, Tina lurched forward in her seat. As the implications of his statement fully sank in, her jaw dropped. Several heartbeats later, she managed to speak. "Y-You're willing to help pay for the renovations?"

He made a show of relaxing, one elbow propped against the passenger window. "Seems only fair if we're going to be living in the house."

Trying for a calm response, she meant to say, "Good," but it came out as a cough.

"That's still the plan, isn't it?"

"I...yes. Sure. B-But would we split the profits of the B and B then?"

"I don't see why," Wyatt said, his tone contemplative. "You'll be handling that on your own. And you won't be sharing in the profits from the ranch. But if you'd rather we just paid rent, we can negotiate that."

That didn't seem fair, especially if she was going to be renting out the bunkhouse, which belonged to them. She shook her head. "No, I...this is just getting more complicated than I'd planned."

"Doesn't have to be. We can talk it over with Rex if you want, draw up some paperwork about how we want to structure things."

"We could do that," she decided, trying to tamp down her elation in order to picture how it all might work.

"I've been thinking," Wyatt said next, enthusiasm entering his voice. "The house needs central air. And you and Ty shouldn't have to share that clunky old bathroom downstairs. You should have private bathrooms like the rest of us. Then we could incorporate the old bath into the laundry room, make it a real workable space. And you could use the storage room for an office. I've poked around in there and haven't found anything worth keeping. Of course, you could always share office space with me."

She hadn't even thought of the storage room, but sharing an office with Wyatt? "Uh. I don't know. That's a lot to think about."

"Well, mull it over. You can decide later." Clearly, the decisions were hers to make.

She couldn't help smiling. For the first time, she felt that it could actually happen. Her dream of providing lodging for War Bonnet visitors and a stable home for her son might actually be feasible.

It had been so long since she'd felt optimism that she almost didn't recognize the feeling, but her mood had lifted significantly by the time she parked the sedan in front of Countryside Church.

If God wasn't listening to her, He must certainly be listening to Wyatt Smith.

Either way, she couldn't be anything but deeply grateful. To both of them. God and Wyatt.

# Chapter Eleven

Pleased that Tina had asked and thanked him for his advice, Wyatt finally relaxed. He'd expected for her to lash out at him for that kiss, but she was obviously as eager to forget about it as he was. Too bad he couldn't figure out how to do that.

Kissing her had been a horrible mistake. One that he'd enjoyed immensely and would repeat again if given the opportunity. He did not expect such an opportunity ever to materialize, not even when she placidly filed into the pew with him and his brothers and took a seat between him and Ryder.

Small sheets of paper were passed around so people could write down their prayer requests, with or without a signature. A typewritten list of ongoing requests was also provided. Wyatt jotted down his request and signed it:

Wisdom to discern God's will in domestic and business matters.
Wyatt Smith

Tina scribbled something onto her sheet. It lay in

her lap for several moments while she looked over the typewritten list. Curiosity got the better of him, so Wyatt surreptitiously glanced at what she'd written, smiling because it so closely mirrored his own request:

Important home and business decisions.

He noticed that she didn't sign her name, but after a moment, she retrieved the pen from its holder once more and added another line:

Favor in family court.

So, she expected the custody issue to wind up in court. He hoped—prayed—she was wrong. Rex had outlined a number of instances in which she could easily lose custody. Wyatt hadn't seen the point in detailing them for her, but he'd been praying about the matter ever since his discussion with the friendly rancher and lawyer. Thankful that she would request corporate prayer on the matter, even anonymously, Wyatt smiled to himself.

The congregation, which numbered about half of those who attended on the average Sunday, stood to sing a hymn. Then the pastor read aloud Philippians 4:6.

"Be careful for nothing; but in every thing by prayer and supplication with thanksgiving let your requests be made known unto God."

He went on to explain that the verse meant have no grievous care for anything; do not be anxious or worried. Instead, those with concerns should take their cares and worries to God and be thankful for what they'd already received.

One of the elders read the prayer requests aloud. As usual, Ryder had submitted an unsigned request for the family of Bryan Averett, the young man who had died while practicing with Ryder back in Houston. Some folks jotted down each request. Some took occasional notes. Others, like Wyatt, committed the requests to memory or merely let them sink in. They were instructed that those who wished to speak their prayers could do so as they felt led. Others could pray in silence. They bowed their heads. A few moments of silence ensued before, one by one, various voices put their petitions and those of others into words.

A few prayed with eloquence. More were simple and direct in their praise, gratitude and requests. Several mumbled and bumbled their way through. Wyatt knew very well that it was all the same to God. He refrained from speaking aloud simply because he wanted to address both Ryder's and Tina's unsigned requests in detail. He added requests that Tyler would find peace and joy in his situation and that Layne Kemp would drop his custody suit and stop trying to alienate Tyler from his mother. Wyatt also prayed that Ryder would let go of his guilt and put Bryan's death behind him.

Wyatt and his brothers had attended prayer meeting only sporadically back in Houston—until the tragic death of Bryan. Wyatt had found real peace and comfort in prayer meeting after that, but he could only hope it was the same for his brother. Prayer meetings always seemed brief to Wyatt, but especially so tonight with Tina sitting at his side, looking as pretty and sweet as any woman could in a simple top and jeans. Just knowing that she was there next to him lifted his spirits.

Scary thought. Especially if he was the only one feeling such things.

Pushing away unwelcome thoughts, he smiled and shook hands with all those around him as he made his way out of the sanctuary, Tina at his side, his brothers trailing them. When they reached the foyer, Tina and Jake went to retrieve the boys from their respective groups. Tina returned with Ann Pryor and her son, as well as Tyler. Donovan's beaming smile made Ty's mulish scowl all the more obvious.

"I'm sorry, but I just can't manage it tomorrow," Tina was saying. "Perhaps in—"

"I never have any fun!" Tyler erupted.

"You know that's not true," Tina corrected calmly. "You and Frankie have been having a great time together. I know you want to play with Donovan, and I'm happy for you to do that, but I cannot take you to Donovan's tomorrow."

"You're mean, and I hate you!" Tyler bawled, tearing off toward the door.

Tina sighed. "I'm so sorry, Ann. He's overtired and…" Her words faded away.

Wyatt stepped in. He couldn't help himself. "We appreciate the invitation, and we'll make sure the boys get together again soon."

"And that Tyler is rested and better behaved," Tina added.

Grateful that she didn't appear ready to take him to task for overstepping his bounds, Wyatt blindly reached for her hand and found it, giving it a comforting squeeze. To his everlasting delight, she held on even after he relaxed his fingers.

"Think nothing of it," Ann was saying. "We look forward to hearing from you."

Wyatt smiled, slipped his hand free and lifted it to the small of Tina's back. Together they walked calmly across the foyer and out the door, which hadn't fully closed when Wyatt softly spoke.

"Do you mind if I have another word with Ty?"

"He listens to you a lot better than he does me these days," she answered wryly.

"He's confused by all the changes. Any boy would be," Wyatt said softly as they moved toward the car. Jake already stood beside the truck with Frankie and Tyler, keys in hand.

"That's what I keep telling myself."

He patted her back consolingly, and she sent him a wan smile.

Wyatt asked Jake to move Tyler's safety seat back to Tina's car. Ty folded his arms and stuck out his bottom lip, pouting angrily, but he didn't argue with Wyatt, who stared at the boy in silence while Jake worked and Ryder quietly buckled Frankie into his seat in Wyatt's truck. After securing Tyler's seat, Jake offered the truck keys to Wyatt, but Wyatt shook his head.

"I'm riding with Tina and Tyler."

Nodding, Jake shot Tyler a sympathetic glance. Wyatt took the boy by the arm and walked him around the car. Rather than wait for him to climb up into his seat, Wyatt lifted him into it. Then he got into the back with Tyler. Wyatt caught a glimpse of Tina biting her lip as she slid behind the steering wheel. Without a word, she started the engine and headed home. Tyler started to cry before they got out of the parking lot.

"Sorry, dude. That's not going to work," Wyatt said evenly. "We've already had this discussion. You are not allowed to speak to your mother with such rudeness and disrespect. Everything she does, she does for you, and everyone knows how hard she works. No Christian man would ever dare speak to his mother the way you did just now, not in private and certainly not in public. Do you realize that Mrs. Pryor thinks you're a brat now? Donovan would never be so disrespectful to his mother. If he did, his father would put an immediate stop to it."

"He would?" Tyler queried, tears dripping off his chin.

"Trust me. I know Dean Pryor, and he's a very nice guy, a great dad who loves his kids, and he would never put up with Donovan back talking his mom."

Tyler's brow furrowed as he thought about that. Wyatt hoped that the boy was comparing Dean's parenting with his own father's, but how sophisticated Tyler's reasoning powers were no one could say. Wyatt's hopes rose when Tyler bowed his head and apologized to his mother without prompting.

"I'm sorry, Mom."

"Thank you, honey," Tina said softly. Wyatt suspected that she was crying, too, but he resisted the urge to reach forward and clasp her shoulder. Instead, he kept his focus on Ty.

"Here's the thing," he said firmly. "If you'd just been patient and polite, I would have offered to take you to Donovan's tomorrow, but I will not reward your rude behavior, so you'll just have to miss this playdate."

Stunned, Tyler reacted with anger. Obviously, being so close to getting the playdate and missing out on it anyway infuriated him. "You're not my dad! You can't tell me what to do!"

Wyatt locked eyes with Tina in the rearview mirror. "I may not be your father, but I am the boss on Loco Man Ranch, and that gives me certain authority. I make the rules." He dropped his gaze to Tyler again. "Do we understand each other?"

Tyler nodded. Wyatt could almost see the wheels turning in his little head as he tried to reconcile this new reality with what he'd known up to this point, but Wyatt couldn't let himself soften. Yet.

"You'll have to earn that next playdate, Ty."

"What does that mean?" Tyler practically wailed, dashing away tears.

"If you behave yourself, treat your mother with respect, speak politely and do as you're told, then we'll set up the playdate. The better behaved you are, the sooner it will happen. Got it?"

"That starts right now," Tina told the boy. "And there's just one way to reply, son."

Tyler flattened his lips, but after a moment he muttered, "Yes, ma'am."

Wyatt smiled to himself when she said, "There are two adults in this car."

Tyler slid a look at Wyatt from the corner of his eye, straightened his shoulders and said, "Yes, sir."

Wyatt patted him on the knee. "You might be surprised how much more often you get your way when you go about it respectfully. Pleasant behavior yields better results. I guarantee it."

Tyler nodded mutely. Wyatt let it rest there. All in all, he was very pleased with how it had gone. He wondered if Tina realized that the two of them had operated as a unit in this. They'd presented Tyler with a united front, and while he might not like it, he had to respect it. They'd given him no other choice.

When they reached the house, Tina went around and opened the back door for Tyler, who didn't make a move until she did so. Wyatt got out on his side and waited while Tina instructed Tyler to go in and get ready for his bath. Then she turned to Wyatt, a soft smile on her face. He had to shove his hands into the pockets of his jeans to keep from reaching for her.

"Thank you," she said quietly. "I know he's not your responsibility, but he looks up to you and your brothers. He has behaved better lately."

"I've noticed. All the more reason to hold firm. Look, I hope you don't think I'm overstepping or that I'm criticizing you. I see that you're doing your best with him and everything else, but it's obvious he needs masculine guidance."

She ducked her head. "I know I've let him get away with behavior that I shouldn't." She looked up then, admitting, "I've just been so afraid that he'd choose his father over me, given the chance."

"I can understand that," Wyatt told her, "but I've learned that kids always respect the better parent and instinctively feel safer when adults maintain control and expect proper behavior. It takes time and effort to make children behave and conform to standards. Kids may not like it, but deep down they realize that parents who don't do the hard work of parenting just don't care as they should."

"In my case," Tina mused, tilting her pretty head,

"I put my own emotional needs ahead of my son's. I've been so afraid he won't love me as much as he loves his father that I haven't been the disciplinarian that Tyler needs me to be. Thank you for helping me see that."

Wyatt shook his head. "I care about Ty. We all do, and we see that you fear for your son's future. That's perfectly natural."

"It is," she agreed, "but it's more than that, and you know it. Tyler and I both change *now*. So. Again. Thank you."

"I just want what's best for you and Tyler. I want that above all else." With a shock, Wyatt realized how deeply he meant those words. When had Tina and Tyler Kemp become more important to him than even his brothers or the ranch?

Tina smiled and stepped close, her gaze moving over his face. Then she went up on tiptoe and kissed his cheek just at the corner of his lips. He held his breath as she turned and went into the house. Only then did he remove his hands from his pockets and suck in a deep breath. And all the while he smiled.

Tyler behaved well the next couple of days, but Tina thanked God when Ann called to invite everyone to a picnic that weekend. She couldn't accept for the Smith family, and she didn't want to undercut Wyatt's authority in Tyler's eyes by accepting for Tyler and herself until she'd discussed the matter with Wyatt. She felt a deep gratitude and comfort in partnering with Wyatt on this. He was so much like Dodd in so many ways. She wondered if he knew that.

When she relayed the invitation to Wyatt, she made

sure to do so in front of everyone else, so they could all have their say. That meant broaching the subject on Friday at lunch.

Wyatt looked to Jake first, who shrugged and nodded. At the same time, Ryder said, "We've all been working hard. A picnic would be a nice break."

Wyatt caught Tina's gaze and held it for several seconds. Smiling as she dished out the meal, she glanced at Tyler before speaking. "The boys have certainly been on their best behavior."

Wyatt smiled at Tyler. "So I've noticed." Tyler brightened and sat up a little straighter. "Ask Ann what we can contribute and what time they want to meet tomorrow."

Tyler almost shot out of his seat in delight when Tina revealed that Dean wanted to meet early so he could take the boys fishing at War Bonnet Lake.

"I think I can find a tackle box and a couple of fishing poles somewhere around here," Wyatt said.

"I hab fishies in *my* room," Frankie insisted. Everyone laughed.

"We're not talking about goldfish, son," Jake told him. "The kind of fish you find in a lake is the kind you eat."

"Fish sticks!" Frankie crowed happily.

They all laughed again, though Tyler looked uncertain.

"Obviously, I should make fish for supper more often," Tina quipped.

"You wouldn't hear any of us complain," Wyatt told her. "We're from the Gulf Coast, remember?"

"You don't complain anyway," Tina replied softly. Wyatt just smiled.

He smiled again the next morning when Tina walked into the kitchen in a sundress. The soft, sleeveless black-and-white-checked dress with a full skirt and a skinny red belt fell to midcalf. Combined with red flip-flops and a broad-brimmed white straw hat, the dress felt pretty and summery.

Sadly, it wasn't quite warm enough to swim in such a large body of water yet. Only Ryder wore shorts. Jake wore a baseball cap with his T-shirt, jeans and boots, but Wyatt stood there in a natural straw cowboy hat. His brothers had teased him about his new wardrobe, but he took Tina's breath away in his pale yellow T-shirt, dark jeans and brown boots. He had shaved, but already the dark shadow of his heavy beard skimmed his jaws, chin and upper lip.

She plopped her white hat onto her head and dipped a knee in a mock curtsy. His smile widened.

"I didn't know a picnic could look that good."

She wrinkled her nose. "It's not too much?"

"Uh-uh." He lifted his gaze to hers. "Perfect."

She wanted to throw herself into his arms, and that very impulse made her step back and break eye contact.

Tyler moved between them then, politely asking, "Is it okay if I ride with the guys again? Please."

"Works for me," Wyatt said, looking to Tina.

She knew that he was asking if he could ride with her again, and she couldn't keep a smile off her face. "I have no problem with it."

Wyatt handed his keys to Jake, and picked up the small cooler containing the strawberry shortcake and lemonade that were the Loco Man Ranch's contribution to the picnic. Tina reached for the old, faded quilt that she had left folded atop the kitchen table, and they all followed Wyatt outside, where he secured the cooler on the back floorboard of Tina's car. She dropped the quilt on top of the cooler while Wyatt moved Tyler's safety seat to his truck. As he buckled the safety seat into place, he muttered, "We really need to get another one of these."

"And a vehicle big enough for all of us," Ryder chimed in, folding his arms.

"Yeah? What would that be?"

"Minivan. Or an SUV with three rows of seats," Ryder supplied.

"And who would drive it?"

"Tina. Or Jake. In fact, I'll buy Jake's truck myself if he wants to go the SUV route."

"Something to think about," Jake said, lifting Frankie into his car seat.

Wyatt looked at Tina, but she kept her expression bland and noncommittal. In truth, she'd felt a little thrill of delight when Ryder had suggested that they needed a vehicle big enough to carry everyone. In a strange way, they'd become a family. Almost.

The Pryors arrived just then. Dean rolled down the window of an SUV exactly as Ryder had described. Wyatt and Tina looked at each other and grinned.

"Y'all want to ride with us?" Dean asked, meaning her and Wyatt. Not even a full-sized SUV could accommodate six adults and four children in safety seats.

Tina waved toward her car. "Our cooler's already loaded."

"We'll follow you," Wyatt said.

Nodding, Dean rolled up the window and swung his vehicle around in a wide U-turn. Wyatt waved at Jake, who slid behind the wheel of Wyatt's truck as Ryder climbed onto the passenger seat. Then Wyatt lifted a hand, gesturing for Tina to get into her car. She thought about it for a few seconds while Jake started the truck and backed around to follow Dean. Reaching into one of the deep pockets of her dress, she pulled out her keys and pressed them into Wyatt's hand.

"Why don't you drive?"

He tilted his head, smiling. "Okay."

She dropped down onto the passenger seat with a deep sigh. The car was warm from the morning sun, but the air felt just right. The relaxation started now.

Wyatt had to slide back the driver's seat and hand her his hat before he could even get in. Dean and Jake were already turning onto the two-lane highway when he started the car. Tina rolled down her window, leaving the air conditioner off, and Wyatt followed suit. He caught up with the others soon enough. When they turned off onto a tree-lined dirt road, the temperature immediately dropped several degrees, but the vehicles in front of them kicked up so much dust that they had to roll up the windows and turn on the air. The red-orange dirt of south central Oklahoma coated all three vehicles by the time Dean brought their little convoy to a halt in a small park beside the lake.

It was a perfect spot with recently mown, fresh green grass and spreading shade trees. A concrete picnic table flanked by benches stood next to a small grill fixed in place atop a metal pole set into the ground.

Jake and Ryder let the kids out and started unloading lawn chairs and fishing gear from the bed of Wyatt's truck, while Ann and Dean pulled boxes and coolers from the back of their vehicle. Ann wore jeans and sandals with a pretty ruffled blouse, making Tina feel that she had overdressed.

Plucking at her skirt, she told herself it was too late to worry about that now. To her surprise, Wyatt reached over and covered her hand with his. When she looked at him, he shook his head.

"Don't ever worry about how you look. Every time I think you can't possibly get any more beautiful, you prove me wrong."

In that moment, she knew she was falling in love with him.

It wasn't part of her plan. It could only complicate matters. But how could she not fall in love with such a man?

How could any woman not fall in love with a man like Wyatt Smith?

# Chapter Twelve

"Can I go fishing now? Pleeease."

Tyler twisted his fingers together anxiously. Impressed that he hadn't just run off after Dean and Donovan, Tina smiled.

"Of course you may."

"A well-behaved boy is entitled to have some fun, I think," Wyatt said, winking at him.

"Just be sure to do everything Dean tells you to do."

"I will!" Tyler vowed, grinning broadly as he ran off toward the lakeshore.

With baby Glory on her hip, Ann wandered by the blanket where Tina and Wyatt sat. "Don't worry about him. I'm going to take this one down to see what all the excitement is about."

"Should I go with you?" Tina asked, slipping on her skimpy shoes.

"No, no. Just sit and relax."

"Can I do anything while you're gone?"

Ann waved that away. "Plenty of time to lay out

lunch when we get back." She leaned forward slightly, repeating her previous advice, "Relax."

Tina smiled. As Ann turned away, however, Wyatt unfolded his long legs and got to his feet. "How about a walk? There's a path over there beneath the trees. Want to see where it goes?"

Nodding, Tina pulled her feet up beneath her. Wyatt reached down a hand. Leaving her hat on the quilt, she caught his hand and let him pull her to her feet. He kept her hand in his as they strolled the narrow pathway. Tina clasped his hand loosely. For some time, they walked in silence, listening to the others chatter in the distance, before Wyatt chuckled.

"I'll be surprised if there's a fish on this side of the lake, considering how much noise they're making."

"I'd just as soon not have to clean any fish myself," Tina replied dryly, and he grinned at her. She got lost for a moment in his dark gaze. More to cover her reaction to him than anything else, she dredged up more words. "Thank you for recognizing Tyler's good behavior."

He squeezed her hand. "Good behavior should be recognized. But maybe I was more interested in walking out with his pretty mama alone than his behavior."

A little frightened by the thrill that his compliments gave her, she scoffed. "Flattery isn't necessary."

"It's not flattery." He sounded a little offended. "It's fact."

"Oh, please."

"Don't you realize how lovely you are?"

Shaking her head, she answered with determined candor. "I'm well aware that I'm overweight."

He stopped dead in his tracks, tugging her around to face him. "Overweight? Where'd you get that idiotic idea?"

Blinking, Tina wished she hadn't brought up the subject. She shook her head, but Wyatt pulled her closer, the dark slashes of his eyebrows drawing together.

"I'm serious. I want to know where you got the ridiculous idea that you're overweight."

Shrugging, Tina told him, "My mother for one. Layne for another."

"Your mother and your husband told you that you weigh too much? That's insane."

Something inside Tina opened, lightened. She felt her bottom lip begin to tremble but refused to allow herself to shed a tear. She'd already cried rivers over this issue.

Clearing her throat, she said, "My mother was tall and slender. I—I couldn't measure up to her ideal. She was telling me that I was too heavy by the time I was ten. That's why I so resented the nickname Tiny." She looked down, adding, "Layne said I was fine until I got pregnant. Then he started saying I was too round. After Tyler was born, Layne complained that I was too curvy."

"Too curvy," Wyatt echoed, rolling his eyes. "Curvy is not overweight. Your curves are perfect. I have no idea what you looked like at ten, but you're certainly not overweight now. How can you look in a mirror and not see perfection?"

Tina couldn't quite accept that, but hearing him say it exhilarated her. Wyatt was very much a man's man, and so handsome that he made female hearts flutter. No one's compliment could have affected her more. Yes, he could be very commanding, but he was also caring, dependable, hardworking and considerate. She'd come to realize how much he carried on his broad shoulders, and no one could deny his fairness and generosity, least of all her.

Stepping close, she confessed, "I misjudged you badly in the beginning, Wyatt, and I'm sorry for that. You're really very—" *wonderful*, *adorable*, *wildly attractive*, but she settled on "—sweet." He grimaced slightly, as if that wasn't what he'd hoped to hear, so she stepped closer still and went up on her tiptoes to kiss his cheek. Embarrassed by the impulse, she turned back to the path, only to find herself pulled around once more by the hand that Wyatt still clasped.

His gaze capturing hers, he stepped into her, his free hand slipping about her waist. Then he simply dipped his head and kissed her. Tina felt small and delicate and treasured. Without even realizing what she was doing, she lifted her arms about his neck. Everything about the kiss felt genuine and cherished.

This was real. This was true. This was what she'd wanted, needed, what she'd been searching for without even realizing it. How could she have settled for Layne's shallow courtship? Hadn't she learned anything from her mother?

Her mother.

She had become her mother, going from man to man.

Appalled, Tina yanked away, stumbling backward.

Wyatt stood there with his arms open, confusion all over his face. "Sweetheart, what's wrong?"

"I—I'm not my mother," she blurted. "I'm not marrying every man who shows interest in me!"

Wyatt's expression clouded, hardened, his arms slowly sinking to his sides. "Who said anything about marriage? I was only—"

Stung, she declared, "Well, I'm certainly not the kind of woman to settle for anything less!"

"I never implied that you were!"

"Isn't that what the mauling was all about?"

"The mauling." He scrubbed his face with his hand. "You are a beautiful woman. I like you. I more than like you. Of course I want to kiss you. That's not *mauling*. And you started it!"

"I did not! I only…" But she had started it. When she'd kissed his cheek, she'd hoped he would do exactly what he'd done. Swallowing the excuse on the tip of her tongue, she raised her chin.

A rustling in the brush at the edge of the tree line caught their attention. Tina turned her head to see Tyler running toward them, a fish dangling at the end of a short length of line.

"Mom! Mom! Look! I got a fish!"

He'd obviously heard their raised voices and crashed through the brush in his excitement to show off his catch. Wyatt was the first to react. Smiling, he examined the fish still dangling from the hook.

"That's a nice catfish you've got there."

"Look at its long whiskers," Tyler said proudly.

Tina's smile felt stiff, but she kept it in place. "Good job, son."

"You'd best get that into the keeper," Wyatt counseled.

"Yeah," Tyler agreed authoritatively. "Mr. Pryor's got a bucket of water special for it."

"Let's go find it," Wyatt suggested, patting the boy's shoulder.

They turned back down the path, leaving Tina to follow. The walk back to the picnic spot took far less time than their earlier stroll away from it, but with every step, Tina's mood sank.

She'd made a fool of herself. Again. What was wrong with her? Was there nothing she couldn't ruin?

Wyatt couldn't believe how foolishly he'd behaved. He relived that kiss and the following argument multiple times over the following days, castigating himself for leaping forward when Tina obviously wasn't ready. He doubted that she ever would be ready, and frustration ate at him, so much so that he couldn't seem to concentrate on any task for longer than a few minutes at a time. Not even the drive to and from a Tulsa-area sale barn and painstakingly culling half a dozen horses from the animals on sale there had kept his mind off her. Rex had asked him more than once what was eating him, but Wyatt had blamed his lack of attention on Dodd's mysterious grass plots.

At the moment, Wyatt was supposed to be helping unload the horses. He'd dropped Rex at the Straight Arrow Ranch and come home to meet Delgado, who had plowed and raked the ground inside the corral next to the barn during Wyatt's absence. Dodd had built the corral of welded metal pipe years ago and it was still sound, so Wyatt and Delgado had merely painted it after readying the stalls in the barn for the horses. Now Delgado was preparing to back the cattle hauler into the corral, and Wyatt was supposed to guide him. Instead, he was staring at Tina, who stood with Frankie and Ty, an arm around each of them, as they clung to the corral railings.

He kept thinking about the wedding invitation that Rex had hand delivered that morning. The moment Rex had mentioned his father's upcoming wedding, Wyatt had thought of Tina.

*I'm not marrying every man who shows interest in me!*

Cut to the quick, he'd lashed out with a crack about no one mentioning marriage. The truth was that he had begun thinking along those very lines. What else could they have between them, after all, if not marriage?

*I'm certainly not the kind of woman to settle for anything less!*

He knew that, of course, and the implication that *he* would settle for anything less than marriage had wounded and infuriated him. He'd long ago determined not to even date any woman with whom he could not at least ponder marriage. Consequently, he hadn't dated anyone in quite a while.

Maybe that was the problem. He and Tina hadn't been on an actual date. Sadly, he didn't see that happening now. Oh, why had he kissed her again? But he knew the answer to that.

He'd kissed her because he'd wanted to.

He still did.

His burgeoning feelings for her had taken over every

part of his life. His prayers revolved around her and Ty. Her needs and schedule took precedence over his. He was even making business decisions based on emotion rather than sound financial planning. He had forked over money to refurbish the house when he should be concentrating on building up the ranch. The reality was that he'd bent over backward to please her, and what had it gotten him? Nothing but heartache.

After the picnic, he'd told himself that he was going to ignore her, but it wasn't possible to completely ignore someone living in the same house, especially when she had to be consulted about so much. Wedding invitations, for instance. He'd told Rex that he'd have to check with the family before accepting for anyone but himself, and to Wyatt's mind, Tina was part of his family.

Delgado beeped the horn on the truck to get Wyatt's attention. Snapping to, Wyatt waved his hand, signaling Delgado to continue backing the trailer toward the open corral gate. Once the trailer edged into the corral itself, Wyatt gave Delgado the signal to stop. Delgado killed the engine and came around to help Wyatt pull out the ramp and open the trailer gate. One of the horses, a silver gray roan that Wyatt fancied for himself, had gotten loose from his headstall and turned around inside the trailer, but the big bay gelding backed down the ramp as if he'd been trained to it before trotting around the corral.

While the roan helped himself to a drink of water, Wyatt and Delgado freed and brought out the other four horses, starting with a handsome red dun with a white blaze and then two more bays, one of them an unusual mouse brown with the requisite black mane, tail and stockings. Just a little darker than a buckskin, the mouse lacked the dorsal stripe that marked buckskins. The final animal was a beautiful copper perlino mare. A very pale gold with a coppery mane and tail, the mare wasn't a small horse, but something about her seemed dainty and feminine. Wyatt had imagined Tina on that horse from the moment he'd first seen it. The perlino was an affectionate thing and nuzzled Wyatt's chest as if looking for pockets that might hide treats. The boys seemed taken with her.

"Ooh, pretty horsie," Frankie crooned, holding out his hand. The mare ambled over and sniffed his fingers, making him giggle.

"What's his name?" Tyler wanted to know.

"*She* doesn't have one that I know of. The big grayish one is called Blue Moon, and the red one over there—" he pointed at the dun "—answers to Handy." The dun picked up his beautiful red-brown head, ears perking. "But none of the others have names yet." He pointed to the light brown bay. "I think we should call that one Mouse because he's a mouse brown."

The boys laughed at that and started debating names for the other bays. They decided on King and Lucky— not very original names, but acceptable. When it came to the mare, however, they were way off base with names such as Whitey and Fizzle. Wyatt pointed out that the horse was pale blonde rather than white and that Fizzle was somewhat derogatory. He suggested Blondie, but Tina nixed that.

"Pearl," she stated firmly. "Just look at her. What other name could you give her?"

"Pearl it is," Wyatt decreed abruptly. Then he silently rebuked himself for catering to the woman's every whim. Yet, he knew that he'd do that and more to get back into her good graces. The problem was he didn't think that possible.

Stark Burns arrived, as previously arranged, to look over the new mounts. A brother-in-law of Rex's, the busy veterinarian had been a great help to Wyatt. Stark had recommended that Wyatt buy Loco Man's starter herd from a single source, then augment with a good bull and sale-barn cows as needed. After much research, Wyatt had purchased one hundred head of Black Angus heifers and calves from a rancher in the northwest part of the state. Delivery would be made in a few weeks.

Parking his truck next to the corral fence, Stark eased his tall, lean body from the cab. He fit his sweat-stained straw hat to his head while shaking out his long legs in great ground-eating strides. It occurred to Wyatt that he was about to lose his best opportunity to speak to Tina about the wedding, so he quickly plucked up his courage and got to it.

"By the way, Rex gave me an invitation to his father's wedding next week. I thought I should talk to… everyone…before I accepted."

She met his gaze for the first time in days. "Ann and Meredith invited me a while ago. I've already agreed to contribute to the wedding feast and decided what to wear."

Of course. Just because he thought of her as family didn't mean she thought of him the same way.

"I see. Well, I'll discuss it with my brothers then."

Nodding, she turned to look at the tall, dark veterinarian. Wyatt made the introductions. Tina couldn't have been more gracious.

"I've so enjoyed getting to know your wife. Can I offer you a cold drink, Dr. Burns?"

"My wife's friends don't call me Doctor," he replied with a smile. "It's Stark. And yes, ma'am, you surely can. I'd roll in the dirt for a drink of cold water."

"We can't have that," Tina said with a chuckle. "And you can forget the ma'am. I'm just Tina."

"Thank you, Tina."

As if an afterthought, she turned her head slightly and asked, "Wyatt? Would you like a drink, too?"

"That would be great. But please include Delgado."

"I'll send out three bottles of cold water," she said, starting for the house. "Come on, boys."

Wyatt helped Frankie to the ground while Tyler hesitated, his gaze locked on the horses milling in the corral. "Go on," Wyatt encouraged lightly. "You can stay and watch after you bring out the water."

Ty shot him a smile and jumped backward, sending up puffs of reddish dust. The boy ran to catch up with Tina and Frankie.

"Frosty," Stark said matter-of-factly.

"What?"

Stark hung his forearms on the top rung of the fence. "The lovely Tina Kemp. According to my wife, you are in hot pursuit, but I detected a chilly breeze in your direction just now. So, what's the deal with you two?"

Wyatt stalled, refitting his hat to his head. He was somewhat shocked that anyone outside the family had put him and Tina together as a couple. Sighing, he wasn't sure how to answer. In the end, however, he gave the other man the truth.

"She's got some issues about her past."

"Ah. Who doesn't?" Stark slipped off his sunglasses and looked Wyatt straight in the eye. "You're looking at the king of baggage right here."

"Oh?"

Stark nodded. "I was married before, you know. My wife and daughter died in a car crash. I felt…responsible, I guess. Because I survived."

"Man, I'm sorry to hear that."

"Took years for me to get past it. If you can get past such a thing. Actually, I didn't move past it at all until Meri showed up. Then it was just a matter of time." Grinning, he slipped his shades back into place and shook his head. "She and Ann say it's just a matter of time for the two of you."

Wyatt looked at the horses. "I'm not sure it's that simple."

"But you wish it was," Stark stated bluntly.

Wyatt made no comment, just dropped his gaze to the ground.

"I'll say a prayer for y'all," Stark said, pushing away from the fence. "If it's meant to be, it'll come right."

Wyatt could only hope, muttering, "Thanks."

"I'll get my gear, and we'll look over these horses. Good-looking animals."

"I'll get the paperwork out of the truck cab," Wyatt answered, turning in that direction. "I've got vaccination records and all that." But his mind wasn't on the horses. All he could think about was Tina.

Together, they could really build something here. If she could trust him enough to give him her heart.

He was very much afraid that she already owned his. Whether she even wanted it was another matter entirely.

## Chapter Thirteen

On the morning of the wedding, Tina dressed with care. The Billings family in general seemed a relaxed, informal bunch, but weddings were important events. She should know; she'd attended enough of them.

Her mother had insisted on traditional weddings with all her husbands except Dodd. Gina had later cited their elopement, rather than her own addiction to the trappings of romance, for the failure of the marriage.

Tina herself would have been happy with a small, informal affair when she'd married Layne, but his parents had insisted on a huge, expensive wedding that had left Tina feeling like a performer in a play rather than a happy bride. Looking back now, she knew that the wedding should have served as a warning about the life she would live with Layne. Everything was more image than reality with him.

She silently prayed that Wes Billings and his bride would have more success building a life together than either she or her mother had ever enjoyed. Wes and Alice were an older couple, and both had been married before and widowed. The idea that they would marry again at this point in their lives puzzled Tina, but she liked Ann Billings Pryor and Meredith Billings Burns, and she wanted to cement her friendships with the sisters, so she'd allowed herself to be drawn into the preparations. Now that the day of the wedding had arrived, however, Tina wished heartily that she could just stay home.

Knowing that she couldn't be that rude, she checked the fit of her bright coral knee-length sheath once more. The snug dress didn't exactly hide her curves, but she felt that the sleeves distracted the eyes enough that she could get away with the fit. Ending at her elbows with a double row of wide ruffles, the sleeves brought a chic accent to an otherwise very simple outfit. Foregoing stockings, she stepped into matching heels before slipping the hooks of coral-and-turquoise drop earrings into the tiny holes in her earlobes. Finally, she fluffed her hair to add fullness, then left the room to help Tyler dress.

Before she reached the door of her son's bedroom, another door farther along the hallway opened and Wyatt stepped out, tugging at his cuffs. He wore a somewhat longer-than-normal black jacket over dark navy jeans and a bright white shirt, as well as a high-crowned black straw cowboy hat.

Dumbstruck, Tina stopped, taking in the handsome man before her. She'd never seen a better looking man. He exuded such masculinity that she felt a quivering of something elementally feminine in her chest. Just as she stared at him, he blatantly looked her over before lifting off his hat and strolling forward. She couldn't make her feet move for the life of her.

As he passed her, he murmured, "Gonna put the bride to shame today."

Smiling at the compliment, Tina stayed as she was until she heard his footsteps on the stairs. Then and only then could she move toward her son's door.

He was playing on the bed when she opened the door, but he immediately hopped to the floor. With Wyatt's image still fresh in her mind, she went to his closet and pulled out Tyler's newest jeans, along with the navy blue jacket of his only suit and a white polo shirt with a soft collar.

"Put these on please." While he changed clothes, she pulled out his best sneakers and a pair of clean socks. Ann had told her that many children would attend the wedding reception and that they'd be given the run of the place.

As she helped him pull on his socks, Tyler smiled and said, "You look pretty, Mom."

"Why, thank you."

As soon as he was dressed, they went downstairs together. The men waited in the kitchen. They were all dressed similarly to Wyatt. Jake even wore a pale straw cowboy hat, but he'd put Frankie in jeans and a striped T-shirt with white sneakers.

"You're a handsome lot," Tina announced, her gaze straying automatically to Wyatt.

"Just trying to look worthy of you," he replied smoothly.

"Don't think we're quite up to snuff," Jake said, smiling.

"You look real good," Ryder added.

Smiling, Tina bowed her head in acknowledgment. "Thank you. Would you load those two big pans of scalloped potatoes into my car? You can use dish towels as potholders."

Ryder and Jake swiped the folded towels from the counter and picked up the pans.

"Mom," Tyler began, "I want to—"

"Ride with the guys," she finished for him, not nearly as upset by the prospect of riding with Wyatt as she should have been.

She fought a spurt of disappointment when Wyatt suggested, "Why don't we fix it so Frankie can ride with you and your mom instead?" Meeting Tina's surprised gaze with his own bland one, he added, "We'll carry the potatoes in our car."

"They need to go to the house, not the church," Tina pointed out, trying not to sound snarky.

"We'll take them to the house and meet you at the church, then."

She nodded, trying to feel relieved, but she just couldn't find the emotion. What she felt instead was keen regret.

The wedding was short and sweet, with Wes Billings and Dr. Alice Shorter vowing that theirs would be a marriage founded on Christian principles.

"Til death do us part," Wes intoned the traditional wedding vow. He then winked at the pastor and quipped, "Considering how long it took me to run her to ground, I'm not about to untie her now."

Everyone laughed, including the bride, whose butter yellow suit complemented the bright yellow roses that she carried and wore in her upswept blond hair.

Tina had made a point of not sitting with Wyatt and his brothers. Murmuring that it wouldn't be wise to let the boys sit together, she'd shepherded Tyler to a narrow space at the end of a pew several rows closer to the front of the church. Using a combination of wisteria and yellow roses, a flowery bower had been created over the happy couple.

After the ceremony, the beaming newlyweds entered a luxury auto and led their guests back to the Straight Arrow Ranch, where a number of neighbors and friends busily laid out a sumptuous buffet to go with the steaks beginning to sizzle on several portable grills. Music poured out into the yard via four outdoor speakers, as children darted about in frenzied play.

Stripped of his wedding finery, which had been replaced with a T-shirt and shorts, Donovan met Tina's car with a big grin plastered on his face. Tina had Tyler leave his suit coat in the car, then kept the boys with her until Jake arrived to grant permission for Frankie to join in the fun. The Smith brothers showed up in their shirtsleeves and were quickly surrounded by chattering neighbors, most of them women. Tina went into the house and found Ann, asking what she could do to help, but Ann shook her head.

"No, no. Not in that dress. I love it, by the way."

"Thanks, but just give me an apron."

"None left. Go and enjoy yourself. Better yet, fill plates for our boys and see if you can get them to eat. If we let it go too long, they'll wear themselves out and be asleep before we can feed them. I'll get you some plates."

Tina went out to round up the boys, her heels sinking into the dusty red dirt. Eventually, she took them off and picked her way barefoot out to where the children ran around in a game of chase. Donovan readily agreed to accompany her back to the house. Tina could tell that Tyler wanted to argue, but he fell in line with Donovan. Frankie was already looking exhausted and ready for a nap, so he didn't balk when she took his hand to lead him inside. After dropping her shoes in a corner, she found disposable plates stacked on the dining table and quickly filled them for the boys, whom she sat on the floor around the living room coffee table.

Jake came in to make sure that Frankie was okay. Seeing that the boys had plates in front of them, he stayed to feed Frankie. The excitement of the day could easily distract even a hungry, sleepy child, so getting Frankie to eat required patience. Wyatt entered the room a few minutes after Jake, talking with Stark, who carried a sizable cardboard box.

Stooping, Stark set the box on the floor, and everyone in the room immediately began oohing and aahing at the trio of fluffy black-and-tan puppies tumbling over themselves.

Tyler gasped and watched enviously as Wyatt reached into the box and examined the puppies one by one. Finally, he held up one with a white face, black eyes and ears and what would soon be a ruff of tan fur. Its body splotched with black and tan, the pup showed white front feet and a curly black tail tipped in white. Wyatt looked the dog in the face then turned it for the boys to examine. It was Tina to whom he addressed himself, however.

"What do you think? Should we keep him?"

Smiling, Tina nodded. Tyler whooped and reached for the pup. Wyatt carefully placed the animal in Tyler's hands. Tyler hugged the puppy to his chest, grinning at Frankie. "We got a dog, Frankie."

Sleepy-eyed, Frankie pointed to the pup. "Pretty."

"What are we going to name him?" Wyatt asked, using a finger to unfurl the tail.

"Curly?" Jake suggested.

"Puppy," Frankie said.

"He won't be a puppy when he grows up," Tyler pointed out. "I think we should call him Tippy."

"Maybe Tipper?" Wyatt suggested.

"Yeah, Tipper!"

The other puppies were quickly parceled out to other guests, Stark explaining that they'd come from a client of the veterinary clinic. As best he could determine, they were a mix of border collie, Pomeranian and coonhound. They'd already received their puppy shots and been weaned from the mother, so they were ready for homes.

Frankie petted the newly dubbed Tipper for several minutes before crawling into his father's lap. Sitting cross-legged on the floor, Jake cradled the boy, whose eyelids drooped lower and lower, despite the cacophony of many voices and music. Donovan eagerly gave Tyler advice on raising the new pup before carrying his emptied plate into the kitchen. Tyler clutched the pup as if he'd never let it go.

Dean came in and took a seat on the couch next to

Wyatt. Donovan returned and sat on the floor between his father's feet, his arms around Dean's legs. Dean stroked the boy's head as he talked with Wyatt about how to train the puppy.

Tyler stood next to Tina, taking it all in, but she saw the desperate envy in his eyes as he gazed at Frankie and Donovan with their fathers and then adoringly at Wyatt. Aching for him, she slipped an arm around his shoulders. Suddenly, he moved away from her. She looked around, catching Wyatt's gesture. Apparently, he had noticed Tyler's envious gaze and beckoned the boy with a simple wave of his hand. Tears glazed Tina's eyes as Wyatt casually pulled Tyler and the puppy onto his lap and looped his arms around them. Smiling and stroking the puppy, Tyler laid his head back on Wyatt's shoulder and listened avidly to Dean's instructions.

At one point, Ty asked, "Will he get to sleep on my pillow with me?"

"When he's housebroken," Dean answered.

"What's that?"

"When he's trained to go outside to use the bathroom," Wyatt explained. "We'll want him trained to work cattle, too. Dogs can be a great help on a ranch."

Tyler hung on every word, but Tina knew it wasn't so much the talk that enthralled him as the puppy and the loving male attention. He was truly one of the guys at that moment, treasured by a man whom he respected.

Tina had to turn away to keep from making a fool of herself. She bumped into Meredith Burns, who insisted that she eat.

"You haven't touched a bite," Meri said, tugging her into a corner, a plate of food in one hand. "Now, you sit right here and eat." She pushed the plate into Tina's hands and pulled over another chair. "I'm not moving an inch until you do." She dropped down onto the chair, smiled and folded her hands.

Laughing, Tina ate and enjoyed a chat with Meredith, even with her mind on Wyatt and her son. She somehow managed to remember the recipe for the scalloped potatoes, which Meredith jotted down on a paper napkin. Then Callie appeared, saying that it was time for the wedding cake. Tina volunteered to help serve.

The cake was actually several cakes of different flavors. Callie had prepared a pretty little two-layer cake for the bridal couple to cut, as tradition dictated. Decorated with yellow roses, it made a lovely display, but Wes and Alice ate the small top layer, and Callie boxed the other one. It would be saved in the freezer for their first anniversary. The guests, meanwhile, were served other cakes prepared and decorated for the occasion by helpful neighbors and friends. Alice made sure to have a photo taken of every cake.

Wyatt showed up at Tina's cake station with an excited Tyler. Knowing her son, Tina immediately cut a piece of chocolate cake for him. Wyatt chose German chocolate.

"Doesn't get better than chocolate, coconut and pecans."

Tyler went off to eat his cake with Donovan at the coffee table, but Wyatt claimed a chair, and began to eat right there at the table while Tina cut cake for others. After finishing, he pitched his trash into the container behind her. Only then did he look at her and ask, "What's your favorite cake?"

"Oh, wow. How to choose? We have everything from carrot cake to lemon and strawberry. But I think the most unusual flavor is a ginger cake with apples in it. I'm saving a piece of that to have with a cup of coffee."

"Mmm, coffee," Wyatt said, glancing around. "Where is it?"

"In the kitchen."

Rising, he headed in that direction. The next thing she knew, she had a steaming cup sitting next to her elbow and Meri was there to relieve her.

"Go. Go," she insisted, all but pushing Tina from behind the small table.

"Don't forget your cake," Wyatt said.

Tina took the plate of cake in one hand and the disposable coffee cup in the other. Wyatt steered her to a spot on the couch. Just as she sat down, Donovan popped up from the floor.

"Dad, will you play soccer with us?"

Dean smiled and hauled himself up off the couch. Tyler looked expectantly at Wyatt, who still stood to one side. Wyatt gave the boy a crooked smile and nodded.

"Leave Tipper in the box, then let's go work off that cake."

Grinning broadly, Tyler placed the puppy on the blanket in the box. "I'll be back to get you soon, boy." Straightening, he grabbed Wyatt's hand, and the pair followed Donovan and his dad out the door.

Ann abruptly dropped down onto the sofa next to Tina, saying, "Those two seem to be getting along well."

Tina reached for her coffee cup. "It's surprising, really. Wyatt's a lot more strict with him than Layne or I. But I'm working on it."

Ann patted her knee. "It's worth the effort. Kids know when you care enough to stand your ground. I had to learn that with Donovan."

Shocked, Tina blurted, "Donovan is a prince."

Ann smiled. "Yes, he is, but he's also a child, and no child is perfect. Once Donovan ran off in the middle of the night with Stark's niece. They were spending the night here, but Meri upset them." She waved a hand negligently. "She and Stark broke up that day, and she was a mess. Anyway, the kids decided to come to our house. Across the pasture. Without telling anyone."

Tina gasped. The Straight Arrow Ranch was almost as big as the Loco Man. "What happened?"

"Meri and Stark found them the next morning. At first, we were too relieved to think of punishing Donovan, especially as Stark and Meri came back from the search with a new understanding between them."

"Wow."

"Crisis has a way of clarifying things, you know. Anyway, we quickly realized that there had to be consequences. The problem was deciding what those consequences would be. I tried to push the decision off on Dean, but he didn't let me get away with that. We decided together, and we enforced the punishment together. And I've been Donovan's 'real' mom ever since."

"Was he not accepting of you before?"

"Oh, he was. He desperately wanted a mom and, being a redhead himself, he figured my red hair made me a prime candidate. But now he knows that I'll do what's best for him no matter what. Just like his dad."

"Dean's a great father," Tina mused.

Ann nodded. "He is. I think Wyatt would be just like him. He's obviously fond of Tyler, and you say his expectations are high."

"Wyatt took care of Frankie while his parents were both deployed," Tina divulged quietly.

"No kidding? A single guy like him? I'm impressed."

"I'm sure Ryder helped out," Tina said. "They all take a hand with Frankie now."

"If you let that get out, you'll have to hire guards to keep the women away," Ann joked.

Long after Ann returned to her duties as a hostess, Tina mulled over that last comment. She was surprised that Wyatt hadn't already married. No doubt he'd had his choice of women back in Houston. He certainly did here. And she was the idiot who kept pushing him away. She winced, recalling her reaction the day of the picnic. Could she be any greater a fool? Wyatt Smith was a rare man. As Dodd's nephew, he'd have to be, but she kept overreacting to his kisses.

How did she tell him that no man's kisses had ever affected her the way his did?

How did she make up for past assumptions and behavior?

A simple apology couldn't begin to mend what she'd broken. But maybe... Just maybe, if God was willing and she could find the courage, she and Wyatt could find a way to get past her stupidity.

## Chapter Fourteen

Smiling to himself, Wyatt watched Tina dust off her feet before stepping into her heels. She'd been barefoot all day. Those heels did amazing things for her legs, but the juxtaposition of that gorgeous dress and the informality of delicate bare feet enchanted him.

He wanted to kiss her while she stood against him in those heels.

He wanted to kiss her while she stood barefoot.

While she chatted with her friends.

While she shepherded the boys.

He wanted to kiss her. Period.

More than that, he wanted her to wish for the future they could have together.

Feeling Tyler slump against him, Wyatt looked down. The boy had utterly exhausted himself. All day he had sought Wyatt's attention and approval, and Wyatt knew perfectly well why. The other kids had dads to watch over them and occasionally join in the play. The way Tyler avidly watched their interactions told Wyatt that he'd never experienced that kind of relationship with his own absent father.

Wyatt wondered if Layne might somehow be encouraged to develop that kind of relationship with his son, and if so, how.

Practically asleep on his feet, Tyler swayed. Even the puppy enthusiastically licking his face couldn't keep his eyelids from sinking.

Reaching down, Wyatt swung both the boy and the puppy into his arms. Tyler laid his head on Wyatt's shoulder, cradling the puppy against Wyatt's chest. Frankie, who had enjoyed a short nap that afternoon and now rode comfortably in Jake's arms, stretched out a hand and patted the dog, giggling when it licked his fingers.

"It's been a long day," Tina observed. "They're both exhausted."

"Let's get them home," Wyatt said.

He and Jake carried the boys to Tina's car and tucked them into their safety seats, while Ryder went in search of the truck. The puppy traveled in Ty's arms. Wyatt suspected they'd have a hard time getting the dog away from him, so he didn't try.

After following Tina's car home, Wyatt sent Ryder to the barn to find a suitable box to use as a crate for the pup. It wasn't yet full night, but both boys had fallen asleep.

Wyatt passed the puppy to Tina, then pulled Ty from his car seat and carried him into the house. After penning the dog up in the laundry room, Tina ran upstairs to change while Jake and Wyatt got the boys ready for their baths. She returned wearing soft knit pajamas and a long robe belted tightly at the waist. Wyatt smiled at her bare feet and left her to shampoo Tyler's hair while he made a bed for the dog with an old blanket and the box Ryder had found.

Jake carried Frankie into the kitchen wrapped in a towel. Ryder helped him dress the boy for bed, and Jake carried him upstairs to bed. When Tina herded a sleepy, cranky Tyler into the room, his footsteps dragging, Wyatt hoisted the boy into his arms.

"Come on, dude. Bedtime."

"My puppy," he whined.

Wyatt nodded at the box on the floor. "Mom will bring him along."

Tyler smiled all the way up the stairs, but he refused to lay down until the dog arrived in its box. Tina placed the box near the head of the bed, and Ty obediently stretched out. The moment his head hit the pillow, he closed his eyes and pretended to fall asleep. When Tina attempted to pull up the covers, the boy grunted a complaint and kicked the covers out of her hands without ever opening his eyes. She looked at Wyatt, a droll smile curving her pretty lips. They both knew that Tyler wasn't really asleep and that he wanted Wyatt to tuck him in but didn't know how to ask.

Thinking of Frankie, who had two uncles, in addition to his father, to love him, Wyatt moved between Tina and the bed. He pulled up the covers and carefully tucked them around Tyler. Then, on impulse, he bent and kissed the boy's temple, just as he'd have done with Frankie. Tyler gave himself away with a smile, but he didn't open his eyes. Tina adjusted the light in the room and followed Wyatt into the hallway.

"What a great day," Tina said softly, pulling the door closed behind her.

"Those Billings know how to throw a wedding, don't they?"

She nodded. "Thank you for spending time with Tyler today, and for the puppy. I've never seen him so happy."

"He's a good kid. He just wants what everyone else around him has."

"He's a *better* kid, thanks to you. I wish…" She shook her head.

Wyatt couldn't stop himself. He reached out and pulled her to him. Soft and feminine, she huddled against him, her arms folded up against her sides, hands pressed to his chest. After silently praying for the right words, he spoke.

"You know, sweetheart, the Billings have it right. Wes joked about it today, but the truth is that true marriage leaves no room for divorce."

She said nothing for a moment, her cheek pressed to his collarbone, her head tucked neatly beneath his chin. Then she pulled in a breath and asked, "But what if you make a mistake?"

"Then you trust God to help you fix it. My folks always said that you both have to believe. Then you put the other first, and together you honor God. If you do that, divorce never needs to be an option."

"But it takes two people to make that work," she argued softly.

"That's right," he agreed. "The key is to choose someone who will work at marriage as hard as you do.

It requires a level of trust that too many people simply ignore before they leap into a relationship."

She sighed and pulled away, lifting her lovely amber gaze to his. Her voice shook as she said, "The thing is, I guess I trust you more than I trust me."

Smiling, Wyatt cradled her cheek with his hand. "Then trust me when I tell you that you're not your mother."

She seemed to mull that thought for a moment. Then she simply walked to her bedroom door. There she paused and hesitantly smiled at him. Then she closed the door.

In that moment, he made up his mind that he was going to give this thing between them his best shot. His very best shot.

When Wyatt woke in the morning, his first thought was of Tina.

How could he help her?

How could he show her how much he cared for her?

He made it his mission to find out over the next few days, observing all that she did and making mental notes. It rained for a couple of days straight, which made it convenient for him to entertain Frankie and Tyler one afternoon so she could watch a favorite program on TV uninterrupted. They played with the puppy, who was quickly learning what was expected of him.

When the opportunity arose, Wyatt sat down with Tina to go over her plans for the house, and consulted with his brothers and Dixon Lyons.

He drove into Ardmore and bought rocking chairs

for the front porch, and every evening after the boys were in bed, he sat next to her, rocking gently as she watched the stars or spoke quietly of her past and her hopes for the future.

He made sure that he was available to watch Ty and Frankie while Tina and Ann drove into Ardmore to have their hair done one day. Afterward, he complimented Tina.

"Looking fabulous. But then you always do."

She looked even better wearing a soft smile and a blush on her cheeks.

When he came down the stairs on Thursday morning of that next week, she was at the stove, dressed in jeans and a neatly fitted cotton blouse. She glanced over her shoulder, smiling.

"Coffee's ready."

"Great. I'll help myself after I set the table."

She turned around, watching him as he went to the cupboard. "You don't have to do that."

"I know. But it's better than sitting at the table watching you work. Not that I don't like to watch you."

She ducked her head, the corners of her mouth quirking as she fought against a smile. Turning back to the stove, she poked at bacon sizzling in the skillet on the burner.

"I've been thinking," Wyatt said, pulling down plates from the shelf in front of him. "I'd say it's time to paint the outside of the house. Wouldn't you?"

For a few seconds, she said nothing. Then she tentatively began to speak. "Lyons will do it, but they can't get to it for some weeks yet. I've been thinking of starting it myself, now that the rotted siding and trim have been repaired. Shouldn't be any big deal to roll on some paint. Can't be that different from what I've been doing inside."

Wyatt carried the plates to the table and set them down before speaking. "I really don't want to see you up on a ladder wielding a paint roller. You pick out the paint. I'll get the house painted."

"The cattle are coming today. You don't have time—"

"I have as much time as you do. At least I'm not homeschooling the cows."

"We'll be done for the summer soon."

"Good. I'm thinking it's time Tyler learned to ride."

Tina turned just as Tyler let out an eager whoop of delight, nearly dropping Tipper in the process. Wyatt hadn't intended to speak in front of the boy, but he hadn't seen Ty enter the room. Frankie came running a moment later, followed by Jake and Ryder.

"I get to ride a horse?" Ty asked excitedly.

"Soon," Wyatt hedged, looking to Tina. "Provided your mom agrees." Tyler's arms were wrapped around Wyatt's waist before he finished speaking, the puppy on the floor at his feet.

"Every boy who lives on a ranch learns to ride horses," Tina said, bending to sweep up the pup and place it in its box. "Every girl, too, for that matter."

"So you ride, do you?" Wyatt asked, grinning.

"Of course. But it's been a while."

"I ride horse, Daddy?" Frankie asked Jake.

Lifting the boy onto his booster seat, Jake smiled. "Sure. Someday."

Happy, Frankie kicked his feet, shifting side to side on the chair. Tina smiled and nodded at Tyler.

"Let's wash our hands. Then you can get the silverware from the drawer."

Tyler released Wyatt and ran to obey. Wyatt shared an approving look with Tina.

"About painting the house," Wyatt pressed gently.

Ryder spoke up. "Jake and I are going to do it. We can rent a sprayer."

Tina beamed as Wyatt said, "I'll buy the paint, then."

Her eyes glistening, Tina spread a soft smile around the room. "I don't know how to thank you all."

"Maybe you can work on the kitchen next," Wyatt told her, glancing at the tired countertops and flooring.

Turning back to the stove, Tina said, "I really hate to give up this old stove. It has so many ovens and burners. They don't all work, though."

"Maybe we can recondition it," Wyatt suggested, stepping up close behind her.

"Th-that would be wonderful," she said brightly, but everyone heard the grateful tears in her voice.

How had he ever thought her cold and prickly?

"Shouldn't be too much of an issue," Jake put in. "I'll look at it after breakfast."

Tina bent her head, obviously overcome, and Wyatt quietly slipped his arms around her from the back. She kept turning bacon in the skillet, muttering that he was going to get burned if he wasn't careful.

"I don't mind," he whispered into her ear. He had to bite his tongue to keep from speaking. Now was not the time to tell her that he loved her.

Sniffing, she asked loudly, "How do you want your eggs, boys? Scrambled? Over easy? Sunny-side up?"

"Scramble!" Frankie yelled, and everyone chuckled.

"Scrambled it is." She turned off the burner and moved to one side, reaching for the carton of eggs on the counter. Wyatt tucked his thumbs into the waistband of his jeans, watching as she took a bowl from the cabinet over her head and began cracking eggs into it.

A throat cleared behind him. He'd forgotten that he had an audience, but he didn't have a problem with that. No secrets here. Pivoting on one heel, he raised a loosely closed fist and tapped his chest, just in case either of his brothers didn't understand how things stood with him where Tina was concerned. Jake lifted an eyebrow and gave him a thumbs-up. Ryder just grinned and headed to the coffeepot.

It was Tyler's stare that most moved Wyatt, however. He'd been pretty tough on the boy, but no one could mistake the hungry, hopeful look on Tyler's small face. Winking at him, Wyatt went to the refrigerator for milk.

Now, if only Tina could return his feelings… It had to be more than gratitude, more than simple partnership.

He went into his day with that silent prayer.

Two eighteen-wheelers loaded with cattle arrived a couple of hours later. Surprisingly, Ty showed up in the barnyard, widely skirting the two idling tractor-trailer rigs.

"Your mom know you're out here?"

His eager gaze locking on the two saddled horses standing in the corral, he nodded. "Yes, sir. I finished my lessons already and took Tipper out."

"Good job. Go stand over by the corral fence and stay there until the rigs pull into the pasture." As he spoke, Delgado swung open the wide metal gate for the trucks. The ranch had numerous passages protected by cattle guards set into the ground, but none of them were wide enough to accommodate big rigs. Only the main gate behind the house was wide enough for that.

Keeping one eye on the cattle haulers and the other on Ty, Wyatt made a decision. While Delgado waved the trucks through the gate, Wyatt asked Ty if he wanted to ride out with them.

"Yes, sir! Please."

"We'll ask your mom. But don't say anything in front of Frankie. I can't put you both on my horse."

Eyes wide, Tyler nodded. They went into the house and found Tina studying paint colors on the computer. She glanced up as they entered the room.

"Is it okay if Tyler rides out with Delgado and me? He'll ride with me on my horse."

"Don't tell Frankie," Ty whispered, lifting a finger to his lips.

Tina pursed her lips against a grin and nodded. "Okay. But you need a baseball cap. Go to your room and get one. Quietly."

"Yes, ma'am." Ty slipped out to do as told.

"He deserves this," Wyatt said, smiling. "I'll take good care of him."

"I know."

"I'll take care of you both," he promised gravely, "if you'll let me."

The corners of her lovely lips curled upward even as her gaze dropped. "I know."

He stood there for a moment, debating with himself. The word *patience* whispered through his mind. Tugging on the brim of his hat, he turned. Walking out of that room without kissing her took more willpower than anything he'd ever done, but Tyler slammed into him before he got two steps away.

The boy righted himself and slapped the cap onto his head. "Ready!" He called to his mom, "Tell Frankie to take care of Tipper for me!"

Wyatt could see a second dog in their future, as Tyler had firmly claimed Tipper as his own. Eventually, Frankie would want the same. Well, it was a big ranch.

Wyatt and Tyler hurried out of the house and crossed to the corral, where Delgado waited on horseback. Wyatt threw Tyler up into the saddle and mounted the big blue roan behind him. They exited the corral through a gate that opened onto the pasture and cantered around to haze and count the cattle that poured from the trailers. With every head accounted for, Wyatt signed off on the transport. Delgado rode back to open the gate for the rigs again, while Wyatt and Tyler drove the herd away from the opening.

When they came to the first of the fenced grass sections, Wyatt climbed down and took a pair of wire cutters from his saddlebag. Dodd had taught his nephews to carry certain supplies with them, especially those needed to repair fencing.

"Might as well start figuring out which of these grass fields is best for our cattle. Right?"

"Right," Ty agreed, as if he actually knew what Wyatt meant.

Explaining as he went along, Wyatt cut the wire

mesh fencing and rolled it back to secure it so the cattle couldn't get caught up. A few head of cattle milled around outside the fence when Wyatt and Tyler rode away, heading back to the house.

What they found there shocked Wyatt. The cattle haulers were gone, but a pair of flatbed trucks and a strange sort of combine had replaced them. Both Delgado and Tina stood in the yard talking with a khaki-clad man holding a clipboard. Wyatt rode into the corral, tied up the horse and lifted Ty from the saddle before walking out into the barnyard. Tina pointed in his direction, and the man turned to meet him, hand outstretched.

"Mr. Smith, sorry to hear about your uncle. I'm Carter Bishop with Guaranteed Sod, Inc." He reached beneath some papers and pulled out a slip. "The check's made out to Loco Man Ranch, so we shouldn't have to rewrite it."

"The check?" Wyatt echoed in confusion, taking the slip of paper. His eyes nearly fell out of his head when he looked at the amount, but he tamped down his excitement. "I don't understand."

"We contracted with your uncle for sod, and we're here to cut now. Unless the crop's unsatisfactory. Our last inspection showed no problems, and he submitted the correct spraying schedule, so—"

"Sod!" Wyatt exclaimed, flapping the check. "Grass sod! Of course!" He shoved the check at Tina. "Sweetheart, look! This is what Dodd was doing."

She took the check, her eyes popping out at the amount. "Oh, my."

"The sod!" Wyatt exclaimed again. "I cut the fence!"

Turning, he ran for his horse, Tyler on his heels and crying, "I can help!"

Wyatt didn't argue. He just threw Ty into the saddle and leapt up behind him. They were tearing across the pasture at breakneck speed in seconds. Only one heifer was grazing on the bright green grass when they arrived. Leaving the horse outside the fenced field, Wyatt bailed off and ran, yelling at Tyler to stand in the gap of the fence.

"Just lift your arms and yell if the cows come close."

Tyler stood in the center of the opening and raised both arms. The heifer spooked and ran in the wrong direction at first. Wyatt turned the critter and drove it back toward the opening, praying that the cow hadn't wreaked too much damage. He yelled at Ty to get back. The boy scrambled aside as the heifer charged through the opening then he resumed his post.

"Good work, cowboy."

Ty beamed.

Turning to survey the field with new eyes, Wyatt could only laugh. Sod. Why hadn't he seen it sooner? He caught Ty, lifted him under the arms and whirled him around, crowing, "God bless Uncle Dodd!"

They quickly repaired the fence with supplies from Wyatt's saddlebags, mounted up and galloped back to the house. Meeting Delgado and the sod cutters on the way, they stopped for a quick discussion. Delgado knew as much about the grass fields as Wyatt did, so he took on the role of supervisor for Loco Man Ranch.

"Uh, just one thing," Carter Bishop said, hanging out the open window of his truck. "Dodd told us he'd have room for my crew to spend the night."

"No problem," Wyatt told him happily. "Bunkhouse will be ready for you."

"We should be out of your hair by tomorrow afternoon," Bishop said.

"Take as long as you need," Wyatt told him, grinning so broadly that his cheeks hurt.

Bishop waved a casual salute and pulled back into the cab. The sod cutter's truck was trundling along behind the other machinery when Wyatt spurred the roan toward the house.

After they reached the corral this time, Wyatt swung down from the saddle and reached for Ty with a smile. To his surprise, the boy wrapped both arms around Wyatt's neck and held on for a long time.

Hugging the boy close, Wyatt said, "Let this be a lesson to you, son. God has ways of fixing things, ways we can't even imagine. All this time I've been trying to figure out what Dodd was doing, and he was raising a cash crop. That's money in the bank, money none of us counted on."

"Cool."

"Very cool." He set the smiling boy on his feet and started unsaddling the horse. "Want to give me a hand with this?"

"Sure."

"Okay. Stay in this area right here." He carefully swung an arm, indicating the safe space, just as Dodd had taught him. Working together they led the horse into the barn and stripped away the tack. "We'll brush him down. Always remember that when working around a horse, you need to keep one hand on him as much as possible. That way he won't get startled and kick you."

"I'll remember," Tyler promised with a nod of his chin. After a moment, he sighed with satisfaction. "It's a good day."

Wyatt chuckled. "A very good day."

Together they groomed the horse, put out extra feed and walked to the house.

Hand in hand.

# Chapter Fifteen

Tina waited for Wyatt and Tyler at the kitchen table. She popped up as soon as they came through the door.

"Everything okay?"

"Everything's great. Can you believe this?"

She shook her head, looking at the check in the center of the table.

"God fixed it," Tyler announced gaily. "He's got ways."

Tina laughed. "Yes, I suppose He does."

Wyatt couldn't help himself. He hugged her. "Everything's going to be fine now, sweetheart. I know it."

She looked up, lifting a hand to his face. "It feels that way at the moment."

He almost kissed her right there in front of Ty. Thankfully, Jake and Ryder showed up with Frankie just then. Wyatt explained the whole situation. Ryder plopped down in a chair and picked up the check, astonishment all over his face, while Jake clapped his hands and laughed.

"Guess this move was the right thing, after all," Ryder said.

Jake clapped him on the shoulder. "God's got it all in hand, little bro. He's got it all in hand."

Ryder smiled up at him. Wyatt stood with his arm around Tina's shoulders, appreciating the scene before him. It had been a long while since he'd seen his family this happy. He didn't think he'd ever felt such delight himself, but he knew it wasn't just that check in Ryder's hand. It had much more to do with the woman at his side, those gathered at the table and this place.

Home.

They were truly home now, all of them.

A thought suddenly occurred to him, and he quickly turned to Tina. "I forgot to tell you. The sod-cutting crew will be staying the night. Is there anything we need to do to get the bunkhouse ready?"

"The beds need sheets. That's all. But what about supper? Do they have their own groceries? Are they planning to go into town? If so, they can't work too late."

Wyatt hadn't even thought of that. "What do you suggest?"

Shrugging, she bit her lip. After a moment, she said, "Tacos. I have lots of ground beef in the freezer, and they're easy to fix for a crowd. I can run into War Bonnet for the rest of the ingredients."

"Sounds good."

Nodding, she hurried to the freezer and began extracting packages of meat.

"Sounds like a party to me," Jake said, grinning.

"Birthday party!" Frankie yelled.

When they stopped laughing, Jake explained, "It's not a birthday party. It's a blessing party."

"Bessing party!" Frankie cried, making everyone laugh again.

"A party means treats," Tina said, moving toward the small table near the door where she kept her handbag and keys.

"Treats!" Frankie shouted, jumping up and down.

She paused to look at Wyatt and Tyler. "Will you be okay here?"

"We're good," Wyatt told her, parking his hands at his waist. He looked down to find that Tyler had mimicked his stance.

"Good," the boy echoed with a nod of his head.

"Yes, you are," Tina said, lifting her gaze to Wyatt's.

"We'll make the beds in the bunkhouse while you're gone," he told her.

"Are you sure?"

"Sweetheart," Wyatt said, "we've been making our own beds for years. Go on. Do what you need to do."

Smiling, she turned for the door. "I'll be back soon."

The instant the door closed behind her, his brothers began teasing him. "Yeah, *sweetheart*, we're old hands at making beds."

"And if we weren't, Wyatt would make us learn."

"Yes, I would," Wyatt admitted with a broad, unrepentant smile.

That and more. So much more. Whatever it took.

The evening turned into a real celebration, especially after Carter Bishop pronounced the sod excellent and urged Wyatt to sign another contract.

They discussed the details around the table in the dining room, and Tina was surprised to learn that only about a half inch of soil was taken with the harvested grass. The root tips and other detritus left behind helped recondition the soil for new planting. Bishop stated that his company had been harvesting and selling sod produced on the same property for as long as forty years. Considering that it paid over five thousand dollars an acre, with Guaranteed Sod doing the cutting, it was a very profitable business. Given the acreage of Loco Man and the preparations already done by Dodd, it seemed like a no-brainer to Tina. But then, it wasn't any of her business. Until Wyatt made it her business.

He reached across the table and covered her hand with his. "What do you think, sweetheart? You should have a say in this. Loco Man Ranch is your home, too."

*Sweetheart.* That endearment was getting to be a habit with him, one Tina wished didn't thrill her every time she heard it. That thrill consumed her to the point that she almost didn't hear Jake and Ryder agreeing with Wyatt.

"We've had our say in the house," Ryder pointed out. "Only fair you should have a say in the ranch."

"You're a part of this, even if it's not formal," Jake put in. Grinning at Wyatt, he added, "Yet."

Squeezing her hand, Wyatt asked, "So, what do you think?"

"I think you'd be foolish not to do it."

He sat back in his chair, freeing her from his clasp. Tina quickly tucked her hand into her lap, telling herself that she was reading too much into the situation.

Tapping the edge of the table with two fingers,

Wyatt said, "It's unanimous then." He smiled at the guest sitting next to him. "You've got yourself a deal, Carter." The two men shook hands on it.

"When your uncle first came to us with this idea, we weren't too sure," Carter admitted, "but he convinced us to sign the contract, and he obviously did his research and picked perfect spots to plant. Given the size of the Oklahoma City market, we couldn't be happier."

"Contract," Wyatt repeated, stroking his chin. "I haven't found a contract anywhere." He snapped his fingers. "I forgot about the safety deposit box. It must be there. I'll check first thing in the morning."

One of the Guaranteed Sod flatbeds had already left. Much of its haul would be on the ground before the second truck left the next afternoon. Because it had rained recently, the sod was perfect for cutting, but Carter warned Wyatt that certain sections, which would be harvested in another month or so, would need a good wetting before he returned with the cutters. Wyatt promised to see to it.

The four extra men at the table ate heartily and complimented Tina on the meal, but the German chocolate cake she'd thrown together with the help of a boxed mix got raves, especially from Wyatt, who ate two pieces. Later, after the sod-cutting crew left for the bunkhouse, he helped her put Tyler to bed, praising the boy for his help.

"You stood in the gap for me today. You're going to make a fine cowboy and an excellent ranch hand."

"Then I can get boots like Donovan's," Ty said happily. Tina traded knowing glances with Wyatt. Not too long ago, Tyler would simply have demanded boots. Now he hinted.

Wyatt pretended to consider. "Hmm. You know, we probably ought to get you a hat, too." Reaching out, he ruffled Tyler's hair.

Tyler beamed so broadly that Tina had to look away to keep from laughing. Her son was flourishing under the influence of Wyatt and his brothers, much as she had done with Daddy Dodd.

She suddenly missed the old man keenly. She should've known that he would look after all their best interests.

As Tyler hugged her good-night, Tina realized that if he ever had to leave here now, it would be the same for him as it had been for her. He'd forever feel that he'd lost his true home and family. He'd forever miss the comfort, caring and wisdom. They hadn't heard a word from Layne since their arrival in War Bonnet, but the threat of a custody battle hovered on the horizon like an angry cloud, and Tina couldn't help worrying about it. As of yet, she had no independent means of support, and Layne would undoubtedly exploit that.

*God fixed it. He's got ways.*

She closed her eyes and said a quick, silent prayer. *Thank You, Lord. Thank You for everything that's happening here. Please fix the rest of it, for my son's sake. And mine. If that means Wyatt and I together... give me courage to accept Your will, whatever it is.*

Tyler lay back on his pillow, and Tina and Wyatt gently tucked the covers around him. Wyatt kissed the boy's temple, and Tyler settled in with a happy sigh, reaching down to pet Tipper in his box and closing his eyes. Tina had little doubt that she'd find Tipper on the pillow with Tyler the next morning, but she didn't mind. After adjusting the light, she and Wyatt left the room and walked down the hallway to the top of the stairs, where he stopped and pulled her into his arms.

"What a day, huh?"

"The best. I'm so happy for you and your brothers."

"For all of us. We can really do up the kitchen now. And I was thinking this evening that the formal dining room could use a more finished look. You've done a good job in there, but I heard something about shutters instead of curtains."

She remembered that conversation. She'd been talking to Rob and Jake as they'd moved the dining-room furniture into place. She hadn't realized that Wyatt had been listening. If she'd known at the time, she'd have been angry at Wyatt's eavesdropping. Now just the fact that he remembered her preference for shutters over curtains touched her deeply. He was a supremely caring man.

Nevertheless, she shook her head. "They'd have to be specially made to fit the windows. I'm not going to spend your money that way."

"Why not?"

"It's not fair, Wyatt. What if we have a falling out and—"

He gave her a quick squeeze. "We're going to fall out, Tina. Not too often, I hope. But it's going to happen. Again." He chuckled. "That doesn't mean anyone has to leave. Let's just settle this right now." He spread his hands against her back "Whenever we butt heads around here, we cool down, and we work it out. Deal?"

What she felt for him spilled over then, swelling up in her heart and flooding every cell of her body. She tipped back her head. "Deal."

She hoped—prayed—that he'd kiss her again. But that wasn't all she wanted. She wanted to know that he felt the same way she did. She wanted to hear him say it. She wanted him to ask her to make this all formal. To her shock, she wanted him to ask her to marry him.

It seemed, for once, that she was on a roll here. Life was good, and she could almost believe that it was going to get better. With Wyatt. Because of Wyatt.

She stood expectantly, as his gaze roamed her face. But then the only kiss he bestowed was to the center of her forehead. Tina tried not to let her disappointment show as he released her and started down the stairs.

That was when she began to pray that both God and Wyatt would ignore her previous protestations and give her the one thing for which she'd vowed never to ask. She wanted to marry again. She wanted to be the wife of Wyatt Smith. It was time to let go of the past, both her mother's and her own.

The next day, Wyatt drove into War Bonnet to the bank, where he was shown the safety deposit box that Dodd had rented. He watched as the bank manager opened the box and left the room. Pulling out the drawer inside, Wyatt carried it to the table in the center of the small vault and lifted the hinged lid. He found copies of the wills on top, followed by a couple of hundred dollars in cash, three slotted folders filled with silver coins and two piles of stapled papers. The first group of papers was the contract with Guaranteed Sod, Inc. The other made him gasp in surprise.

Standing at the waist-high table, he scanned the pile of documents. Then he rolled up the papers and tucked them under his arm. He left the wills and the money in the box and returned the drawer to its slot, closing the lock face and removing the key, which he tucked into a pocket. Then he hurried home, laughing and praising God for His generosity.

When he got to the ranch, he had to look for Tina. He found her in the bunkhouse making beds and generally cleaning up after the sod cutters. He tossed the papers onto the bed, saying, "I take back every unkind thought I've ever had about Uncle Dodd. The man was a genius."

Turning, Tina smiled at him. "You found the contract."

"Oh, sweetheart, that's not all I found." He reached around her and picked up one of the stapled stacks. "Take a look at this."

She gingerly accepted the papers and began to scan them. "Dodd sold the mineral rights."

"To raise money for the sod, I think. But he didn't sell the mineral rights. Those belong to you. He sold the right to exploration and drilling. Look here." He folded back several sheets and pointed.

"They start drilling in June!"

"That means they've done the survey and they're pretty sure they've got oil and natural gas on Loco Man." Tina blinked at him. "It's got to be out there." He flung out an arm. "It's two thousand acres of Oklahoma, one of the richest oil and gas fields in the world!"

"Royalties," she whispered, clearly stunned. "It's going to pay royalties."

He cupped her face in his hands. "You're going to have ample income, you and Tyler. You don't have to worry anymore."

"God fixed it," she whispered.

"He's fixed it all," Wyatt confirmed, grinning broadly.

"Almost," she said, her eyes glazing with a faraway look. "All that's left is Layne and the custody suit." She crushed the papers to her chest and squeezed her eyes shut, tears leaking from their corners.

Wyatt knew that, even as she silently rejoiced, she'd give every cent of Dodd's gift, everything that she owned, to keep her son safe with her. He wrapped his arms around her and kissed her forehead.

"God's got this," he told her. "God has it all in hand. I know it."

She rested her head in the hollow of his shoulder. "I believe. I do. I believe with all my heart."

Exactly one week later, God put that belief to the test.

It had been a lovely week, despite a sudden and unexpected tornado warning that had everyone on the place crowding into the cobwebbed cellar out back of the house. Tina had clasped Wyatt's hand as he'd held a trembling Tyler on his lap and prayed for the storm to dissipate without injury to anyone. After that, Frankie had started playing with the flashlight, eliciting laughter with the funny faces that he'd made. Tyler had gotten in on the act. By the time the thin wail of the tornado siren in town had signaled the all clear, Tipper was happily chasing the flashlight beam and the boys were reluctant to leave the cellar. Now, remembering how they'd frolicked across the yard, making faces at one another, Tina smiled out the open window above the kitchen sink.

The outside temperatures continued to rise, so they would soon have to close the house for the summer and turn on the new air-conditioning unit. Tina found herself reluctant to do so, but she recalled how hot Oklahoma summers could be. No matter the daytime temperatures, she hoped that she and Wyatt would continue to sit out on the porch in the evenings. Often, they failed even to speak, but just sitting there with him brought her a delightful peace.

So much had happened since she'd come back. She could hear the boys laughing upstairs. As she washed the breakfast dishes that morning, her thoughts wandered from the coming summer and the boys to the dishwasher Wyatt had ordered and the shutters that Dixon Lyons was building, not only for the dining room but the parlor, as well. Lyons and Son would begin the attic and den remodel on Monday. So much for which to be thankful.

Closing her eyes, she mentally repeated the same personal prayer she'd been praying the past week.

*Father God, how I thank You for all You've done. Give me wisdom, and make Your will clear to me. If Wyatt is Your will for me, help him see my love and teach us how to grow a strong, permanent relationship. If that's not what You want for us, give me the strength to let go of that dream. To Your glory and in the holy name of Your Son. Amen.*

When she opened her eyes again, she saw, through the window screen, a car turn into the yard. She didn't have to look twice to know who had arrived. Horrified, she recognized Layne's flashy red convertible all too well.

At first, she froze. Ryder and Jake were outside painting the house, however, and the instant Layne got out of the car, Layne addressed them. Pushing back the sides of his trendy sport coat, he splayed his hands across his ribcage just above his waist and looked up at them through the lenses of his expensive sunglasses, his blond hair gleaming in the morning sunlight.

"This the Loco Man Ranch?"

"That's right," Ryder answered.

"Is there a woman named Tina Kemp here? She might be using some other name. She's about this tall." He held up a hand at about shoulder height. "Short brown hair and brown eyes. There's a boy with her."

Frightened, Tina dimly became aware of two things simultaneously: the boys were playing in Tyler's room upstairs and the Smith brothers were coming down the ladders. Panicked, even her breathing suddenly hurt. She felt as if her world had just crashed around her.

Then she heard Jake ask, "Who wants to know?"

Her gaze sharpening, she watched Layne's slow, smug smile. "Her husband."

Instantly enraged, Tina slung water from her hands and flew to the door. Yanking it open, she pushed through the screen door and stepped out onto the narrow stoop, parking her hands at her waist.

"My *ex*-husband," she stated, loudly and clearly. "What are you doing here, Layne?"

Not that she had to ask. She knew perfectly well why he'd come. What she didn't know was what he hoped to accomplish. Taking a deep breath, she sent up a silent prayer.

*I believe. You've got Your ways, Lord, and You can fix anything. I believe.*

From the corner of her eye, Tina noticed that Ryder took out his cell phone and turned away, but her own focus targeted Layne like a laser.

"Thought you could take my kid and hide, did you?" He slid a glance around the place, his nose wrinkling. "I thought even you had better taste than this, though."

Tina let the insult roll off her as she had countless others, feeling a calmness settle over her.

"We're happy here, Layne. This is where we're staying."

He chuckled, scuffing the toe of his Italian leather shoe in the dirt. "You can stay. I couldn't care less what you do. But my son goes with me."

Panic flashed over her again, but she widened her stance, refusing to show it. That was when she heard Wyatt.

Striding from the barn, he raised his voice, saying, "You'd better be armed with a custody order from the State of Oklahoma, then. Otherwise, Ty's not going anywhere."

Layne whirled to face Wyatt. "Who the—"

"Wyatt Smith."

"And just why should I care who you are?" Layne sneered.

Ryder stepped closer. At six feet three inches, Ryder stood just as tall as his brothers, but he was heavier due to the bulk of his muscles. Anyone could tell just by looking at him that he was amazingly strong. Not once had Ryder wielded that strength in a threatening manner, however. Until now.

Frowning, Layne turned to Tina once more. "Just what's going on here?"

"None of your business."

"Who are these men?"

"We're the Smith brothers," Wyatt answered. "This is our ranch."

Layne goggled at Tina. "And you're living here with one of them? Or *all* of them?"

Before she could respond, Wyatt chuckled dryly. "Oh, that's rich. You were caught cheating, and you dare to throw accusations on *her*? Guess that corresponds with all the lies you've told your son about her."

Layne's expression hardened. "Where is my son? I want to see him."

"You'll see him," Wyatt countered easily, "but you're not leaving here with him unless you have a court order mandating that we turn him over to you, and I don't believe you do. Our attorney would have been notified of any court dates or decisions."

"'*Our* attorney?'" Layne parroted sneeringly.

Wyatt looked at Tina, smiling. "That's right. *Our* attorney. Tina is a valued business partner. And a complete lady."

"'A valued business partner?'" Layne mocked. "Only if you value stupidity. And a lady?" He raked a scathing gaze over Tina. She refused to react. "That's a laugh!"

Wyatt shook his head and looked at Tina again, his gaze as warm as the sun shining down on them. "She's beautiful and compelling and bright, and one of the classiest women I've ever met."

"So, you're the one she's shacking up with," Layne crowed. "Well, you're welcome to her. Play house all you want. I couldn't care less. She's not worth the effort, though, I warn you."

Once that might have wounded Tina, but she watched Wyatt's hands curl into fists, and her heart swelled. She almost spoke out to ask him not to hurt Layne, for fear of losing Tyler's affection, but then Wyatt's hands relaxed. She should've known he would keep his cool.

"No one's 'shacking up' or 'playing house' here," Wyatt said calmly. "We all realize that Tina deserves nothing less than marriage and complete fidelity, both of which she could have in a heartbeat. Whenever she's ready to marry again. Given past experience, her reluctance is entirely understandable."

Layne lost every shred of his urbane, charming veneer then, demanding, "Get my kid out here. He'll tell you what a failure she is as a mother and wife. And he'll beg to leave with me. You'll see."

Suddenly, the screen door behind Tina creaked, slapping her in the shoulder as it was flung open. Tyler flew past her, down the steps and straight at his father. Tina's heart dropped—until she realized that Tyler's fists were flailing at Layne.

"Liar! You're a liar! She's not a bad mother! You're a bad father!"

"Whoa." Wyatt caught the boy by the collar, pulling him away from his stunned father. Shaking him gently, Wyatt admonished him in a soft tone. "Hey. That's uncalled for. He's your dad. Be respectful." He cupped Tyler's face in his big hands. "You know how to be respectful. You do it every day around here. With me and your mom, Ryder and Jake, even Frankie."

His face crumpling, Tyler threw himself into Wyatt's arms and sobbed out, "I'm sorry."

"I know." Wyatt patted his back. "But I'm not the one you owe an apology."

Sniffing, Tyler stepped back and turned to face Layne, muttering, "I'm sorry."

Wyatt patted the boy's shoulder approvingly, and Tyler turned a teary smile over his shoulder at him. Layne suddenly reached out, snatching Tyler by the forearm and pulling him toward his car. Tina gasped and started down the steps.

"Come on. Let's go."

"No!"

She halted as Tyler jerked free of Layne. Wyatt stepped up to make sure that Layne couldn't snatch the boy again, wrapping an arm across the boy's upper chest. As Tina let out a relieved breath, Layne resorted to wheedling.

"Don't you want to come with Dad? It's what we've talked about. We'll have fun, buddy. You'll see."

"I'm not going!"

"You don't want me to spend Father's Day all alone,

do you?" Layne cajoled, bending to bring his face level with Tyler's.

"You don't have to spend Father's Day alone," Wyatt interjected, looking down at Tyler. "You're welcome to come back and spend Father's Day with your son. At church and then here on the ranch. But you'll keep a civil tongue and you won't be taking him with you."

"You don't tell me when and where I can see my son," Layne snarled.

"No, but his mother does, and what she says goes."

"According to who?"

"Me. My brothers." Jake and Ryder nodded at that. "And our attorney. You see, he read the current custody agreement, which you did not contest when it was implemented. It states clearly that she has complete custody and your visitation with her son is based entirely on her wishes. Funny how your only objection at the time concerned child support, which—correct me if I'm wrong—you do not pay."

"She agreed to it," Layne pointed out sullenly.

"And you agreed to the custody arrangement," Wyatt retorted. "Wonder what changed your mind."

Tina knew perfectly well what had changed Layne's mind about the custody agreement: Tyler had finally gotten old enough for Layne to use him against her.

"I miss my son," Layne sniffed.

"So come see him," Tina said, looking at Tyler. "We'll work out a visitation schedule so you can see each other as often as you like."

"Oh, you'd love that," Layne snapped. "Having me at your beck and call."

"I'm willing to work with you, Layne. I always have been. We'll schedule visits at your convenience."

"*My* convenience? This isn't about my convenience. When I agreed to have him, you promised he would never inconvenience me, and it's been nothing but inconvenience since the first time he kicked in the womb!" Layne threw up his hands. "And it just got worse and worse after we brought him home from the hospital!"

Realizing belatedly how that sounded, Layne switched his gaze to Tyler, who looked as if he'd been struck. Tina doubted that her son even understood the full implications of what his father had just revealed, but Tyler was smart enough to comprehend instinctively that Layne hadn't really wanted him.

Pinching the bridge of his nose, Layne attempted to make reparations. "Hey. That was then, you know? This is now. We're buddies now. Right?"

"Frankie and Donovan are my buddies," Tyler whispered, mentally putting it all together. As the implications settled into place, he backed closer to Wyatt, stumbling slightly over Wyatt's big, booted feet.

Wyatt tightened his arms around the boy, crooning softly. "It's okay. Don't worry about any of this. It doesn't change anything." Tyler nodded solemnly. Then he suddenly whirled and threw his arms around Wyatt again.

Layne angrily rolled his eyes. "Oh, forget it. You're not worth the effort. Either of you. I'm done!" He stabbed a finger at Tina before waving his hands in a slashing motion. "I'm done with both of you."

"Layne," she began, knowing how that must hurt

their son, but Layne had already whirled and yanked open the door of his car. "Wait," she entreated. "Let's talk." But the only sound was that of his car door slamming shut.

After that, he started up the engine, backed the car around in an angry scatter of gravel and dust, and drove away so fast that his tires squealed when he turned the corner onto the highway. As the red-orange dust settled around them, Tyler sobbed. Tina ran to him, wrapping her arms around him and Wyatt both.

"Don't cry, baby," Tina pleaded, going down on her haunches. "He didn't mean it. You'll see him again."

"He's just upset," Wyatt added. "He'll cool down. Tell you what. We'll write to him, invite him back again to visit. How would that be?"

Sniffing, Tyler rubbed at his eyes with both fists. Finally, he nodded, letting out a weak, "Okay."

"Give him time," Wyatt counseled. "He'll remember what a great boy you are and how much he misses you. He said that. Right? He said he misses you."

Tyler nodded again, his breath hitching repeatedly. "Yeah."

"There you go," Tina said encouragingly.

Suddenly, Tyler threw his arms around her neck. Both thrilled and brokenhearted, Tina hugged him. "I love you so much, son. I'm so proud of you."

"I love you, too, Mom," he said, bringing tears to her own eyes.

He pulled back as Wyatt said, "Someone needs to go check on Frankie."

"I will," Tyler declared, squaring his shoulders.

Jake moved forward then, offering his hand. "I'll go with you."

Tyler took Jake's hand, flashing a weak smile up at him, and the two moved toward the house. At the same time, Wyatt reached down and hooked his hands under Tina's arms, pulling her up and against him. She buried her face in the curve of his neck and let the tears flow, his arms tightening until she could barely breathe.

Tina didn't know where Ryder disappeared to, but when she lifted her head again, she and Wyatt were alone. Wiping her face with both hands, she calmed herself enough to say, "Thank you."

To her surprise, Wyatt spun away, bringing his hands to his hips and twisting with agitation. "I wanted to strangle him. I wanted to wrap my hands around his throat and throttle him. If he wasn't Tyler's father..."

Realizing how much self-control he'd just displayed, Tina's love doubled. She went to him and gently placed her hands on either side of his strong neck.

"You know," she said through a smile, "I would consider marrying again. If the right man asked me."

Wyatt's face went blank, his gaze searching hers. Then he let out a whoop, wrapped his arms around her waist and swung her in a circle. "Thank God. Thank God!"

Tina laughed, threading her arms around his neck. "Is that the proposal?"

He set her on her feet. "I love you. I want to marry you more than anything else in this world."

"I love you, too. I think I have almost from the beginning, but because I've never really felt it before, I didn't know."

Beaming, he asked, "Is that a yes?"

"It's a yes," she confirmed, laughing when he hugged her so hard her feet lifted off the ground. "But let's keep it between us for now. Tyler's had so much come at him today. I think he needs a little time to adjust."

Wyatt nodded, bringing his forehead to settle against hers. "Whatever you want. Just don't keep me waiting too long."

"I promise."

Standing there within the safe, loving confines of his arms, she knew that God had just answered her prayers.

*God will fix it. He's got ways.*

The third Sunday of June brought a blessed silence. No saws buzzing, hammers hammering or sanders screeching.

The work had gone quickly, and Tina could not complain about the quality. The old house felt solid and strong, with modern conveniences and upgrades. More and more Loco Man Ranch felt like home, but the reality far surpassed what she'd envisioned.

Wyatt, who had run upstairs to grab his forgotten Bible while the others loaded into the brand-spanking-new full-sized SUV now parked in the yard, came pounding down the stairs. He'd already had the concrete pad poured for the extended carport that would soon provide shelter for their vehicles. Tina had concentrated on planting flowerbeds and landscaping. Already green shoots were poking through the dirt. Soon flowers would blossom.

Smiling at the thought, she felt Wyatt's hand in the fold of her elbow. As he pulled her around to face him, her smile grew.

He stepped close and lowered his head to kiss her.

Leaning into him, Tina gave herself to the kiss. They'd stolen every moment alone they could these past couple of weeks, and her love for this man had only grown. She'd begun planning their wedding in her mind. She wanted a quiet church ceremony, perhaps in the evening. They'd show off the house at the reception afterward, nothing too ostentatious, just appetizers and cake—unless Wyatt preferred something else. She'd ask him. Later.

A scraping sound reached her ears, but she didn't immediately identify it. With the door hinges freshly oiled and the screen door on a hydraulic arm that automatically closed it to keep it from banging shut, she didn't even think about anyone joining them. Until Tyler let out a yell.

"Whoa!"

Breaking apart, both Tina and Wyatt stared at him, stunned. The grin on his face signaled his approval, but neither of them were prepared for what he did next.

Shoving open the screen door again, he shouted, "Guys! Mom and Wyatt got married! Like Mr. Wes and Dr. Alice."

"We're not married," Tina hastened to correct.

"Yet," Wyatt added, slipping an arm about her waist and pulling her to his side. He smiled down at her. "But soon. Right? That is, if you'll still have me."

Considering that Tyler was hopping up and down with excitement, she saw no reason to delay further.

"I'd be a fool," she told him, "not to take what God has given me."

Wyatt was hugging her and laughing, her feet dangling off the floor, when Jake and Ryder pushed through the door.

"What's this?" Jake asked.

At the same time, Ryder said, "About time. You two haven't been fooling anyone, you know."

"Okay, okay. We're engaged. In fact—" Wyatt reached into his jacket pocket and brought out a diamond ring "—I've been prepared for this moment for some time."

Laughing with delight, Tina let him slip the ring onto her finger. "It's lovely."

"You're lovely," Wyatt said, kissing her quickly. "Now, about the wedding date, I am firmly against long engagements."

Tina's smile was so big it hurt her cheeks, but she couldn't tame it, not that she wanted to. "Now that you mention it, I've always wanted to be a June bride. If you're all right with a small wedding…"

"Ready, willing and able," he declared, folding her against him again. But then he released her. "Ty, what do you think? Will you mind having me for a stepdad?"

Tyler flew across the room, throwing himself against the pair of them. "Now I got a whole fam'ly. A dad and a cousin and uncles. Wait'll I tell Donovan!"

Wyatt picked him up and hugged him. Laughing and crying at the same time, Tina looked around her.

She was home at last, financially secure with a business still to launch and a man who loved her and her son, who was happier and safer than he'd ever been.

She had good friends and more family than she'd dared hope for, and maybe eventually Tyler would have at least one sibling.

Even prayers she hadn't yet prayed were coming true.

She thought of Daddy Dodd and how God had set this plan into motion long ago through him. What else could a woman be but thankful?

"Let's get to church," she said through her smile.

She had some praising to do.

And she couldn't wait to tell Ann and Meri her news.

Or to be Mrs. Wyatt Smith.

\* \* \* \* \*

Dear Reader,

Most of us have had to start over at some point in our lives. This world often throws us curves and catches us unaware. Nothing, however, catches God unaware. Even when our own poor choices cause us to start over, He is ready with a plan. We can rest assured that He never allows anything into the lives of His children that will not serve the best interests of all involved. Of course, we must exercise our free will and get with the program.

That's what Tina and Wyatt find themselves doing, struggling to get with the program. It's clear they each must start over in life and where that new start should begin. Just how intertwined their new lives should be, though, is a mystery—until they get their individual suppositions and baggage out of the way. Isn't that always the struggle?

May your struggles be brief and your trust in Him absolute.

God bless,
*Arlene James*

"I've got trouble, Clarabelle."

The cow didn't answer her. Bethany pitched a forkful of hay to the family's placid brown-and-white Guernsey. "The bishop has decided to send Ivan to Bird-in-Hand to live with Onkel Harvey. It's not right. It's not fair. I can't bear the idea of sending my little brother away. We belong together."

Clarabelle munched a mouthful of hay as she regarded Bethany with soulful deep brown eyes.

"Advice is what I need, Clarabelle. The bishop said Ivan could stay if I had a husband. Someone to discipline and guide the boy. Any idea where I can get a husband before Christmas?"

"I doubt your cow has the answers you seek, but if she does I have a few questions for her about my own problems," a man said.

Bethany spun around. A stranger stood in the open barn door. He wore a black Amish hat pulled low on his forehead and a dark blue woolen coat with the collar turned up against the cold.

The mirth sparkling in his eyes sent a flush of heat to her cheeks. How humiliating. To be caught talking to a cow about matrimonial prospects made her look ridiculous.

She struggled to hide her embarrassment. "It's rude to eavesdrop on a private conversation."

"I'm not sure talking to a cow qualifies as a private conversation, but I am sorry to intrude."

He didn't look sorry. He looked like he was struggling not to laugh at her.

"I'm Michael Shetler."

She considered not giving him her name. The less he knew to repeat the better.

"I am Bethany Martin," she admitted, hoping she wasn't making a mistake.

"Nice to meet you, Bethany. Once I've had a rest I'll step outside if you want to finish your private conversation." He winked. One corner of his mouth twitched, revealing a dimple in his cheek.

"I'm glad I could supply you with some amusement today."

"It's been a long time since I've had something to smile about."

*Don't miss*
An Amish Wife for Christmas *by Patricia Davids,
available November 2018 wherever
Love Inspired*® *books and ebooks are sold.*

www.LoveInspired.com

# Get 4 FREE REWARDS!

## We'll send you 2 FREE Books plus 2 FREE Mystery Gifts.

**Love Inspired®** books feature contemporary inspirational romances with Christian characters facing the challenges of life and love.

FREE
Value Over
**$20**

---

**YES!** Please send me 2 FREE Love Inspired® Romance novels and my 2 FREE mystery gifts (gifts are worth about $10 retail). After receiving them, if I don't wish to receive any more books, I can return the shipping statement marked "cancel." If I don't cancel, I will receive 6 brand-new novels every month and be billed just $5.24 for the regular-print edition or $5.74 each for the larger-print edition in the U.S., or $5.74 each for the regular-print edition or $6.24 each for the larger-print edition in Canada. That's a savings of at least 13% off the cover price. It's quite a bargain! Shipping and handling is just 50¢ per book in the U.S. and 75¢ per book in Canada*. I understand that accepting the 2 free books and gifts places me under no obligation to buy anything. I can always return a shipment and cancel at any time. The free books and gifts are mine to keep no matter what I decide.

Choose one:  ☐ **Love Inspired® Romance**
Regular-Print
(105/305 IDN GMY4)

☐ **Love Inspired® Romance**
Larger-Print
(122/322 IDN GMY4)

Name (please print)

Address     Apt. #

City     State/Province     Zip/Postal Code

### Mail to the **Reader Service:**
**IN U.S.A.:** P.O. Box 1341, Buffalo, NY 14240-8531
**IN CANADA:** P.O. Box 603, Fort Erie, Ontario L2A 5X3

Want to try two free books from another series! Call 1-800-873-8635 or visit www.ReaderService.com.

Looking for inspiration in tales
of hope, faith and heartfelt romance?

Check out **Love Inspired**® and
**Love Inspired**® **Suspense** books!

**New books available every month!**

---

**CONNECT WITH US AT:**

Facebook.com/groups/HarlequinConnection

 Facebook.com/HarlequinBooks

Twitter.com/HarlequinBooks

 Instagram.com/HarlequinBooks

 Pinterest.com/HarlequinBooks

ReaderService.com

LIGENRE2018R2